I0627864

Atlantic City's Most Wanted #8

Charity Parkerson

Punk & Sissy Publications

Copyright

—Warning: This book is intended for readers over the age of 18. Some of my books contain allusions to past abuse and trauma.

CONTENTS

INTRODUCTION

AJAX'S LIFE BELONGS TO the Royal Guard. Being his prince's personal bodyguard is his greatest honor. What is he supposed to do with Lucas?

There are very few select people—still alive, anyhow—who know Prince Noir runs Atlantic City. Lucas used to be proud as hell for being one of those people, and then it almost got him killed. Now he's trapped, recovering in the

1

prince's home. Everything about the situation has him frustrated beyond words. The only thing saving him from disappearing is Noir's sexy general. He isn't sure that's enough.

It isn't in Ajax's DNA to feel remorse or pity. Unfortunately, being involved in something that almost killed Lucas has him feeling things. Despite the age gap between them, Ajax has thought of Lucas as his best friend since not long after they met. Lucas is funny, wicked, and caustic. Everything Ajax loves. Now he has a bad feeling Lucas plans to take his smiles and run. He can't let that happen. If he does, Ajax will be the one who has to kill him.

General is the eighth book in Charity Parkerson's Atlantic City's Most Wanted series. These are sexy and sometimes dark stories where the richest and most dangerous men in Atlantic City meet their match. These are best enjoyed when read in order.

Prologue

THREE MONTHS EARLIER...

It was supposed to be a routine collection. That was all Lucas could think as he moved through the back alley, searching for his prey. This motherfucker had pulled a knife on him before he saw Lucas had a gun. Now the bastard was hiding. Lucas would find him, and then no one else would. What had he expected to accomplish anyhow? Lucas ran drugs for Prince Noir. No one escaped that guy.

4

Even though no one actually knew—other than Lucas and a few more heavily trusted people—that Noir was who ran Atlantic City, they knew someone did. They knew Lucas worked for *the* drug lord here. Surely this guy knew there was no escape. He had to know he was dead.

Lucas carefully picked his way through the trash-littered alley. It was so dark, he could barely see a thing. A solid blow landed on his back. Lucas swung around. When he did, the worst pain he had ever experienced cut through him. Before he could recover, the gun was knocked from his hand. It was dark. He couldn't see where it had gone. Lucas fought, landing a few good blows. Each time he was hit in return, the pain was excruciating. Something warm trickled down his back. It hit Lucas. He had been stabbed. Every blow had actually been a knife plunging into him. He couldn't remember how many times he had been hit, but he was weak. Another punch hit his ribs. Lucas went down. He hit the pavement hard enough to knock what little air he possessed from his lungs. Each time he gasped, it rattled. While shock came for him, he watched his prey vanish again. His mind raced. All he could think about was his mom. He was supposed to be on his way to her so they could celebrate Christmas. It was supposed to be a simple job. This would break her heart and probably kill her. She was in bad health and depended on Lucas to take care of her. What would happen to her now? Maybe Noir would take her in. The thought of Noir had Lucas struggling to reach his phone while he gritted his teeth through the pain. He had to live long enough to beg Noir to make sure she didn't end up homeless.

Lucas somehow managed to find Noir's name and hit the call icon. His vision blurred as he stared at the screen and listened to the ringing.

"Prince Noir's residence. How may I direct your call?"

Lucas coughed. He tasted blood. "It's Lucas. I'm down."

"Lucas?" At the familiar sound of Ajax's heavily accented voice, Lucas' eyes fell closed in relief. Noir's longtime general of his Royal Guard was Lucas' favorite person. He was the only person who could hold his own while bantering with Lucas.

Another round of coughing hit. "Help." It was the only word he could manage.

"I'm on my way. Stay on the phone with me. I'm tracking your location. Just hang on."

Lucas closed his eyes and tried his ass off not to cry. Ajax was coming. If he couldn't save Lucas, no one could.

CHAPTER ONE

PRESENT DAY...

Ajax winced every time he watched Lucas move. He knew it had been three months, and Lucas was probably bored as hell, but he wasn't fully recovered. The type of internal injuries he had suffered, and actually died from shortly, wasn't the type of thing people healed from in no time. The doctors claimed it could take up to a year before he was completely on the mend. Still, his stubborn ass wouldn't rest.

A loud huff left Ajax as Lucas climbed from the bed again. "What now? I've checked on your mom. She's fine. The last I looked, she was beating Lazarus at Gin Rummy." Personally, Ajax found that hilarious. The prince's husband was a deadly contract killer. Yet he played cards with Lucas' mom, Wendy, while laughing uproariously as if there was nothing he would rather be doing. Ajax couldn't stop. "If you're hungry, I'll call the kitchen. If you're bored, just tell me what I can do."

Lucas' red hair was a mess. He had one leg out of the bed and stared at Ajax with laughter flashing in his amber eyes. "I need to take a piss. Do you plan to hold it?"

Rather than backpedal, Ajax never broke eye contact. "If you need me to, then yes."

A loud snort burst from Lucas, followed by a wicked-sounding chuckle. "While I prefer to hit the restroom alone, you can hold it any time you like."

Ajax couldn't stop smiling. "I probably should one of these days. It's a little sad, knowing I'm the only person on the planet who hasn't touched your dick."

Laughter rumbled from Lucas on his way to the bathroom. Even after the door closed, Ajax couldn't stop smiling. Things had been this way since he'd met Lucas several years ago. They played off each other well. Ajax's entire life had been dedicated to duty. While there were other guards he liked, he was their general. He couldn't be true friends with any of them. Lucas was the only person who didn't look at him and see his boss, even though—technically—he was. While Noir ran Atlantic City, Ajax was his right hand. Everyone who worked for Noir answered to him. Ajax didn't think Lucas truly bowed to anyone. He would never give up being his own person. Ajax's smile fell. Right now, that ideology was a bad thing. Every day, he saw Lucas turn a little more calculating. Lucas knew why he had been attacked. He knew where the fault lay, and he wasn't wrong. Ajax had a sick feeling in the pit of his stomach. Lucas was about to grab his mom and run. Then Ajax would be the person Noir sent to kill him.

The bathroom door opened. Lucas' hair was combed. He looked ready to drop. Ajax shot to his feet and swept Lucas from his. It was ridiculous how light he was now. He had lost too much weight. Unfortunately, he still couldn't eat much.

"I've got you. It looks like I should've held your dick after all. The weight obviously broke you."

The tired-sounding laugh from Lucas that was barely audible had Ajax grinding his back teeth. Lucas was young and vibrant. He deserved to be those things, goddamn it. Lucas hadn't been born into this life. He should be on the beach, getting plastered with people his age. Life had been incredibly unfair to Lucas. Ajax wished like hell he could fix it.

"I'm sorry."

Ajax's gaze shot to Lucas' face at the apology. "What?"

Lucas looked sad. "Your jaw is flexing. I'm sorry. I know this isn't what you want to be doing. It's okay if you want Mom to sit with me for a while."

Ajax tried calling his emotions under control while tucking Lucas in. "I'm not angry with you. There's no place I'd rather be. I'm outraged on your behalf." He left it at that. Ajax knew Lucas would blame himself if he kept going.

A bright but obviously fake smile lit Lucas' face. "Okay. You can give me a sponge bath later."

Ajax wanted to laugh, but he couldn't. Every second he saw Lucas weak, bitterness grew inside him. He couldn't stay silent any longer. Ajax was too angry. He was sick of watching Lucas fade and know he might not survive next time.

"Why did you choose this life?" The question came out harsher than he meant, but Ajax couldn't stop. "I know you take care of your mom, but fuck, Lucas. You could've done anything else. You could've had a real life. Now you've thrown it away." He knew he had fucked up by the way Lucas' features hardened. No signs of the laughing boy existed.

Lucas' eyes flashed with rage. Lucas snorted so hard, it had to hurt. "You don't know shit about the real world. All you've ever known is a cozy life. Do me a favor? Get out your phone and search for jobs in this area. Then search for apartment prices. Not a damn soul can make it these days alone, and I have my mom to think about. She worked her ass off her whole life to keep a roof over my head and clothes on my back. The least I can do is the same for her now that her health is failing. So don't talk to me about real life because you don't know shit about it. Sitting up here in your fancy-ass house, you don't know a goddamn thing."

The pure vitriol in Lucas' tone had Ajax straightening away from the bed. He closed down his heart. Feeling any sort of pity always ruined everything. "I'll send your mom."

He heard Lucas' put-upon sigh as Ajax headed for the door. Ajax didn't slow. Now that Lucas had shown exactly how much he resented their association, he wouldn't press his company upon him. It wasn't as if he could change the past. Lucas' choices were made a long time ago. Ajax was only a reminder of that.

The backs of Lucas' eyes burned. He hated that he had lost his temper with Ajax. Ajax was his only friend, really. He didn't deserve Lucas spilling his animosity all over him. It wasn't Ajax's fault Lucas had been born poor, and all his savings was likely gone after three months of being bedridden and auto payments draining his account. They had likely lost their apartment by now and would be sued for the lease violation. The only thing he imagined he hadn't lost was his car, since it was paid for, but Lucas didn't even know where it was. He had driven it the night he was attacked. Lucas was out of touch with everything. He hadn't seen his phone. Lucas assumed it had gotten lost in the shuffle as well. Being trapped with zero insight into the outside world had him half out of his head.

The bedroom door opened. Lucas closed his eyes and pretended to be asleep. As much as his mom was his whole world, Lucas couldn't talk to anyone right now. He was too furious over how life had turned out. Having Ajax point it out made the whole situation even worse. Ajax was the only person who made him feel his age. He turned twenty-seven in a couple of months and all his youth felt like it was lost to him. Lucas stood on a ledge right now. It wouldn't take much to push him over. Life had been too damn hard. Too bloody. He felt three times his age. Lucas honestly didn't want to do this anymore, but he couldn't leave his mom behind. He was all she had. Lucas swallowed past a lump in his throat. There was no out. He was trapped. Lucas felt a stare boring into him. He opened his eyes and found Ajax sitting at his side. His steely gray eyes looked every bit as exhausted as Lucas felt. He blurred as tears filled Lucas' eyes. Lucas quickly looked away.

"I'm sorry."

At Ajax's quietly spoken apology, Lucas' gaze snapped back to Ajax's ridiculously handsome face.

A sad smile touched Ajax's lips and fell away just as quickly. "I got halfway down the hall and deflated." Ajax's hand ran across Lucas' stomach as he leaned over and rested his chin on his other arm on the bed. He held Lucas' stare. "I hope you know I'm not blaming you for anything. This entire situation just has me ready to tear apart the world. You didn't deserve this."

He was so incredibly flawless. His eyes were so light, Lucas swore they cut to Lucas' soul. Jet black hair with streaks of silver that looked like a lion's mane made him look distinguished. The two days' worth of growth on his face made him look slightly more human. He always made Lucas want to touch him, and he didn't know why. Still, secret attraction aside, he couldn't let Ajax believe his own words.

"But I did deserve this. Bad things eventually happen to bad people."

Instead of flying into another rage, Ajax lightly stroked Lucas' stomach. "Doing what you have to do to survive doesn't make you bad. It makes you human. In fact, in my opinion, it makes you better than most. You'd be surprised how many people out there would've left their mom to figure it out alone. You didn't. I think you're incredible."

The words warmed Lucas' chest like nothing ever had. It was nice to have someone look at him like he wasn't a monster, despite knowing everything he had done.

"I've always thought of you as my best friend."

A smile exploded across Ajax's face at Lucas' humiliating admission. "I'd say that's sad, but you're mine too."

Lucas couldn't help his bright smile. He would survive another day... no matter the cost.

CHAPTER TWO

IN MORE WAYS THAN Ajax cared to admit, Noir was scary as fuck. While he was a great prince and an amazing artist and storyteller, he was also totally insane. Ajax had seen Noir do things even Ajax wouldn't do. That said a lot. He could be downright terrifying. That was why he extra appreciated moments like this. Noir sat on the veranda with Lazarus. They enjoyed their breakfast in nothing but their robes. A smile tugged at Ajax's lips as he watched them play footsie beneath the table. Most people might be bored by this daily duty of standing in silence at his prince's beck and call. Not Ajax. He had watched Noir grow into a man. Insanity aside, Ajax loved him the way he would his own son.

Noir motioned for Ajax to sit with him.

Ajax didn't hesitate to claim a seat at the table. Food appeared in front of him.

"Eat," Noir said, pointing toward Ajax's plate with his fork.

Ajax dutifully took a bite.

As he chewed, Noir gave a nod of approval. "Good. Now, have you had a chance to speak with Lucas about living here permanently?"

Ajax swallowed. "No, your highness. I haven't been to see him yet this morning."

Noir nodded. "My attorney has been keeping an eye on Lucas' finances, making sure he's paid and all that. I'm not one to fuss about money, but we're not talking about mine. It's ridiculous for him to continue paying bills for no reason. Plus, I can keep a better watch on him here and Wendy has more people to help her."

"She's adored here," Lazarus cut in.

"That too," Noir agreed.

Ajax hid a smile. It was wild to see two such hardened murderers fall in love with the idea of a good mom. Neither man had one of those. Ajax enjoyed seeing them find a chosen mom after all these years. It helped that Wendy openly adored everyone. She acted like everyone under this roof was one of hers. It had taken barely a week for her to claim her spot as matriarch.

"I'll speak with him today." He already heard Lucas' rejection ringing in his ears. Lucas wouldn't want to stay here forever.

Wendy pushed her walker onto the veranda. Her assigned guard slash caretaker, Izaak, stayed closely glued to her side. Wendy was all smiles. "Good morning."

Lazarus stood and pulled out a chair for her. "Good morning. How are you today?"

Wendy accepted Izaak's hand to help her sit. Her light green eyes flashed with life. She looked every bit as nice as she was. It was easy to think of her as older than her forty-three years. A chronic illness had destroyed her health. But when she was in the room, it was hard to reconcile the sight of her. She looked much younger than her age. Wendy was incredibly beautiful with her long, braided red hair and light green eyes that matched her son's. It was as if the walker shouldn't exist, but it did. Ajax was angry with life on her behalf.

"I've been with Lucas all morning," Wendy said, pulling Ajax from his thoughts. "The nursing staff came by and helped him shower and whatnot." She focused on Ajax. "He's completely wiped out now. When I left, he was dead to the world."

Ajax quietly ate and listened to Wendy talk about her plans for the day. He saw right through her, and Ajax couldn't look away once he saw her game. She carefully plotted her day so Ajax would be with Lucas for the next several hours. The way her knowing gaze kept flashing his way told the entire story. She was matchmaking. It was cute.

"Did Lucas have breakfast?"

Ajax perked up at Lazarus' question. Lucas hadn't been eating enough.

Wendy shook her head. "He fell asleep before he could eat."

Noir looked his way. "You should take some food to him and make sure he isn't disturbed."

Ajax pushed from the table and stood. "Yes, your highness." As always, like a well-oiled machine, a full plate of food appeared alongside a glass of juice. Ajax accepted both with a dip of his chin in thanks. Once he was out of sight, Ajax picked up the pace. He didn't know how long it had been since Wendy left Lucas' room. But the guy was stubborn enough to be up dancing, for all he knew. Lucas lived to push too hard.

Ajax quietly entered the room.

Lucas still slept peacefully.

After setting his haul aside, Ajax removed his dress jacket and draped it over the back of a chair. He had learned from months of dealing with Lucas every day, there was only one true way to keep him in bed. Ajax circled the bed and toed off his shoes. Then he gently climbed in beside Lucas. On his side, he studied Lucas's sleeping face. He truly was a work of art. It was no wonder people lined up to fill his bed. The strawberry-blond hair and light green eyes combined with the smattering of freckles across his face and his full lips. He was flawless. They were friends. Ajax didn't want to notice those things. He couldn't help it. Some things were too blatant to ignore. Lucas' sex appeal was one of those things.

Lucas shifted.

Ajax closed his eyes and pretended to sleep.

Lucas covered him with his mound of blankets and scooted closer until he snuggled against Ajax.

Like always, Ajax took a deep breath and enjoyed the stolen moment. Sometimes, he liked to pretend Lucas belonged to him. It was a secret fantasy just for him. Lucas would never want someone like him. He was too old. Too enmeshed in the crime world. Lucas wanted to escape. He was happy with whatever Lucas gave. Anything at all would be enough.

Damn. Ajax always smelled like a dream. Lucas loved cuddling against Ajax's chest. He wanted to be closer. Lucas slipped the buttons loose on Ajax's shirt. There was no way Ajax was comfortable in his dress shirt while trying to sleep. The moment he could, Lucas slid his arm beneath the material. Unfortunately, Ajax also wore an undershirt. That didn't stop Lucas from snuggling even closer.

Ajax's hand slid across Lucas' bare side until he reached Lucas' back, lightly holding him. His lips pressed against Lucas' forehead and then moved to Lucas' cheek. Their breathing turned harsher. The air changed. It was as if they waited to see who would break first. Fuck it. Everyone knew Lucas was easy. He turned his head, capturing Ajax's lips. Heat and passion exploded through their kiss. Holy hell. Lucas didn't know what he expected. This was so much better than anything Lucas could dream.

The door suddenly opened.

Ajax rolled from the bed and landed on the floor.

Lucas looked toward the door. He knew he had to look exactly like he had been sleeping hard before being disturbed.

Izaak poked his head into the room. For a moment, he looked confused. "I thought

Ajax had been ordered to stay at your side today?"

Lucas looked around, trying to look more confused than panicked. He didn't want Noir to take Ajax from him. His gaze landed on the bathroom door. Never had he been more thankful a nurse had pulled the door closed earlier.

"Um." He swiped his hand across his face. "He's in the bathroom."

Izaak nodded. "Okay. Prince Noir has ordered for you not to be disturbed today, but Wendy." He paused for a second, as if catching himself. "Your mother has asked me to let you know she's going out for sunshine and fresh air."

Lucas nodded. "Okay."

"She asks that you text her if you need anything."

"I don't have a phone."

That seemed to give Izaak pause. "Oh. I suppose have Ajax text her."

Lucas nodded, doing his best to look ready to go back to sleep, because really, he wanted to go back to sleep.

Izaak turned the lock on the door. "I'll lock this behind me, then. That way, you'll be left to rest."

Lucas gave him a thumbs-up.

Izaak pulled the door closed.

Lucas peered over the edge of the bed, finding Ajax relaxing with his fingers linked behind his head and his ankles crossed. He couldn't help the smile that exploded across his lips at the sight of Ajax. "Well, well, General Ajax. Dereliction of duty. What would your prince say?"

"He'd probably ask if you live up to the rumors."

Lucas rolled onto his back and roared with laughter. Ajax was genuinely his favorite person. Lucas never tired of him.

Ajax popped to his feet. He peeled his dress shirt off and then his undershirt. Lucas watched him fold the items before setting them aside. Ajax's sexy smile swung Lucas' way as he climbed back into bed.

"You look like you're having a hard time staying awake. Close your eyes." Ajax tugged Lucas into his arms to snuggle.

Damn. Lucas wished like hell he felt better. Ajax had kissed him, though. Lucas wouldn't let him have any peace now. At least, not until Lucas had what he wanted: the sexy general straddling his hips, crying Lucas' name.

Chapter Three

The walker had a built-in seat. Just like his mom's. It was depressing but oddly freeing. Ajax made him walk laps around the room. He sat when the exhaustion beat him and then went back to walking when he caught his breath. Ajax sat on the edge of the bed, looking like a proud papa. Of course, he had shown up with the walker, so he probably patted himself on the back with each one of Lucas' turns. Lucas was the one who had to do all the damn walking. He knew he needed to regain his strength. Lucas genuinely didn't want to stay stuck in bed forever feeble. He just hated all this work to do things he had done his entire life. It was bullshit. He wanted his life and freedom back. Lucas felt like a prisoner trapped inside his own body. That was the one place there was zero chance of escape.

But then Lucas's gaze would lock on Ajax, and he felt an odd pang of... something. It was like all his senses lit. He smelled liberation.

As Lucas pushed his walker toward Ajax, a luminous smile lit Ajax's features. "You're looking chuffed to bits right now."

"I always look this way. You know I'm cocky."

Ajax chuckled as he helped Lucas steer the walker as closely as possible to Ajax.

Lucas sat.

Ajax helped him turn the walker to face him and pulled him even closer. Once he had Lucas where he obviously wanted him, Ajax ran his hands up Lucas' thighs. "I'm not sure it's cockiness if you live up to the hype."

He felt the smirk that stretched his lips. The reaction was out of Lucas' control. He had always been naughty all the way to his soul. Everyone had a talent. His was being very good at being bad. At the moment, Ajax was the forbidden fruit. Lucas wanted to taste him.

"Oh." Ajax leaned back and reached into the inside pocket of his jacket. "I have something for you." He passed Lucas a phone. "No luck finding your old phone. I bought you a new one. It's unlimited everything and on Noir's dime, so go wild."

Lucas tried to not wince. Another connection to Noir. Every day, it looked less and less likely he'd ever escape this mess.

"Thank you." Lucas turned the phone on and worked to set it up. By the time he had signed into all his accounts, he already had a message waiting. Lucas clicked on the message. A smile exploded across Lucas' face. Ajax had sent him a gif of a penguin running at him like it intended to hug him.

Lucas shook his head. "You're one of a kind, for sure."

A light knock landed on the door before Ajax responded. The short warning gave

Lucas just enough time to push his walker with his feet and away from Ajax before Izaak stuck his head inside the room. "You have a visitor, Lucas."

That confused the fuck out of Lucas. He didn't have friends beyond Ajax and—as far as he knew—no one knew he was here. "Uh. Okay. Send them in, I guess." Even to his ears, Lucas sounded unsure.

Kash strolled into the room, looking exactly like the badass he was. "Hey! Look at you. You live. I had started thinking otherwise since you haven't bothered to call."

Lucas couldn't help his smile. Kash was such a come and go guy. Lucas never knew when he was in town. When he was, it was usually bad news for someone. "Hey, Kash. I'd say the phone runs both ways, but this is my first time touching a phone in months." Lucas motioned toward the phone as he made the claim.

Ajax stood and squeezed his shoulder. "I'll let you visit with your friend. Text me if you need anything."

"Okay." Lucas couldn't help the way his gaze followed Ajax to the door. As Ajax passed Kash, Kash nodded at him, but didn't acknowledge Ajax in any other way.

Kash didn't speak again until they were alone. "The general of The Republic of Serveno, huh? That's a hell of a guard. How did all this happen? I heard you were stabbed a few months back, but I never expected all this."

Lucas used the last of his energy to shift from the walker into the bed. He didn't respond until he was covered and caught his breath. "Yeah. It seems I died and everything, but here I am."

Kash's features hardened as he sat in the chair next to the bed. "Who do I need to kill?"

A smile snapped to Lucas' lips. "Rumor has it he didn't make it through the night, but who knows? You know how rumors are." Lucas would not incriminate anyone or substantiate any stories. Lucas wasn't a snitch, and Lucas had never been sure where Kash's loyalty really lay.

Kash didn't call him on it. "Do you at least know who attacked you?"

Lucas didn't like this conversation. "Honestly, I don't remember much about that night at all. I know I stopped somewhere on my way to celebrate Christmas with Mom, and I didn't make it."

Kash shook his head. "That's crazy. How is your mom, by the way?"

The subject let Lucas' smile turn real. "She's doing great, actually. Noir took us in, and she's got all the guards smitten with her. They dote on her and take her everywhere. My guess is she'll refuse to leave when the time comes. Hell, Lazarus might not let me take her. It seems he's claimed her as his own."

Kash smiled. It didn't dim throughout Lucas' speech. "I don't doubt it. There aren't that many genuinely nice people in the world. Your mom is one of them."

Lucas nodded. He couldn't take it. Kash hadn't come around in the three months Lucas had been at Noir's. "What brings you by today?" He kept his expression as friendly as possible. Kash might be playing nice, but that could change any second.

Kash shrugged. "I just hadn't seen you around for a while. So I put out some feelers and heard about what happened. Everyone talks like you're still on death's door. I had to see for myself."

"Nah. I'm still kicking, but I'm always happy to see you." Lucas did it without thinking. His gaze slid down Kash's body like second fucking nature. Being a flirt had gotten him through life. It was how he had met Noir, by blatantly flirting with a prince as if he had a single shot. Even though Noir had been new to this country and only seventeen, he had already been more terrifying than anyone Lucas had ever met. Lucas hadn't let that deter him. Noir was sexy as hell with all his over-the-top confidence. He was so polished and serious, Lucas never would've dreamed Noir was younger than him, much less only seventeen. Noir had been impressed by his nerve and ability to speak to anyone, making them adore him. He was a chameleon.

The smile the slowly stretched Kash's lips proved he wasn't immune. Kash winked. "You should definitely get better soon. I've always got time on my hands...and stamina."

Goddamn it. If Lucas knew how to do one thing, it was paint himself into a corner. Now all he could do was brazen things out.

Lucas' expression turned sultry. He felt it happen. "You should hang out for a few."

So Lucas could figure out how in the hell he would weasel out of this.

The way Kash's lids hooded didn't give him hope. "I'm not running."

Fuck. Lucas felt too bad to be the one who ran. It might be a long day.

Kash fucking Humphries. Ajax hated the bastard. He loathed the guy's stupid, sexy face and wicked personality. For one thing, he was younger than Ajax, as in closer to Lucas' age. He always looked right through Ajax—like he knew Ajax could never compete. But Ajax had money, soldiers, and the ability to make that motherfucker disappear. He would too if that Lothario laid a goddamn finger on Lucas. Ajax would snap his thick neck.

"Whoa. I'd hate to be the person who caused that look."

Ajax didn't calm at Noir's laughter-filled words. He filled a wingback chair in Noir's private sitting room. Ajax hadn't even checked to make sure he wouldn't interrupt an intimate moment. Those happened a lot in this room.

Instead, Lazarus read Noir's latest book while massaging Noir's feet. He tossed a glance Ajax's way. "Fuck, dude. Who pissed in your coffee this morning?"

Ajax didn't humor the pair. He was too angry. "Why in the hell is Kash here?"

Noir looked confused. "Someone has had to cover for Lucas while he's been

CHARITY PARKERSON

down. Speaking of which, have you talked to him yet?"

Damn. He had been a little distracted by Lucas' sexy personality. "I had literally just opened my mouth to do so when Kash arrived."

Noir's confused expression didn't lessen. "What were you doing all day yesterday?"

Ajax had been with Noir since Noir had been a child. He had his poker face down to a science. "Exactly what you ordered me to do. I let him rest. He's been walking around the room, trying to get stronger. Yesterday, he pushed too hard and slept all day. He'll never heal properly if I don't let him rest when he needs it."

Noir sighed. It was a put-upon sound. "I expect you to speak with him today. As much as I'd like for him to choose to stay,

48

I'm not above forcing the matter. Lazarus has never had a good mother. I'm not keen on the idea of him losing Wendy. You know nothing comes between me and spoiling my husband."

Ajax was likely the only person alive—besides Lazarus—who ever questioned Noir's decisions. "Is Wendy even aware you've unilaterally decided to keep her—like a new pet?"

Lazarus chuckled but stayed glued to his book.

Noir rolled his eyes. "Of course we discussed it. She's happy here. There's way more help to give her more freedom. But she insists her decision will hinge on Lucas, so get him on board... no matter what it takes."

Not a single thing could show exactly how spoiled Noir was better than this entire conversation. Ajax wasn't sure he even saw other people as real. Thankfully, Ajax fully intended to keep Lucas and wasn't above using every dirty trick in the book. He held Noir's gaze and smirked. "No worries, mate. You know I can do this." His smile vanished. "But Kash needs to move along. He's definitely trying to undermine me."

Noir made a dismissive motion. "You're free to focus solely on Lucas for as long as it takes. Tell Kash I'm impatiently waiting for him to get to work. That should send him out the door."

Ajax stood. He bit back his triumph. Kash would only be here if he was a guest of Noir. Now Ajax had been given permission to kick him out. "With pleasure, your highness." Ajax felt his face hardening on the way back to his man. His man. Ajax liked the sound of that. He hadn't planned to move on Lucas. Ajax had genuinely expected to carry his infatuation to the grave. Now Lucas had kissed him, and all bets were off. Lucas would be staying. Ajax planned to ensure it. No pretty boy could beat him. Ajax had experience on his side. In truth, he held all the cards.

CHAPTER FOUR

HE WAS GONE. AJAX'S heart crept into his throat. The wheelchair that usually sat in the corner was missing too. Surely Lucas hadn't gotten far. Ajax turned, determined to do whatever it took to get Lucas back. His heart rate dropped a hair. Kash pushed Lucas toward his room. Lucas was all smiles.

Ajax wanted to punch Kash in his perfect face.

Kash's dark blue eyes flashed with challenge and humor. He knew Lucas could be his.

Ajax kept his features smooth, falling into his role as the General. "Kash. Just who I was looking for. The prince has kindly asked you to get to your assigned duties. He grows impatient for results." Ajax practically felt Lucas' confusion, but Ajax kept his gaze locked on Kash. He needed Kash to understand. The time to leave was ten minutes ago.

Kash grunted out a low laugh. "Let me get this one back to bed and I'll gladly get started."

Lucas steered his way out of Kash's hold. "Don't worry about me. I've had lots of practice getting into beds."

If Ajax wasn't mistaken, there was a hint of relief in Lucas' voice. Ajax's gaze dropped to Lucas. Sure enough, he wanted to be out of Kash's clutches. That was all Ajax needed to know to turn his mood around.

Unfortunately, Kash wouldn't be that easily escaped, it seemed. Kash moved in step with Lucas' wheelchair until they were all shuffled into the bedroom. Much to Lucas' obvious displeasure, Kash didn't stop trying to touch Lucas as much as possible until he had Lucas tucked beneath the covers. Then he swiped his lips across Lucas' cheek.

"See you later, sexy."

Lucas' smile was so brittle, Ajax wondered how many teeth cracked while trying to hold on to the grin. "You know where I'll be."

Kash finally straightened and headed for the door. Ajax stepped aside to let him pass and Kash smirked. It had been a long time since he truly wanted someone dead. Now Kash topped that list.

The moment they were alone, Ajax closed the door and then locked it on the sly. When he turned, he found Lucas covering his face with both hands. It took Ajax a second to realize he wasn't crying. He laughed so hard, no sound emerged. His body shook in the silence. Ajax's smile was out of his control. Lucas had such a fun and sexy personality. He made the world brighter.

Ajax peeled off his dress jacket and draped it over the chair in its usual spot.

He slipped the buttons loose on his shirt. "I have to know. What's so funny?"

Lucas swiped his eyes. He barely got himself under control enough to answer. Laughter laced every word. "Is that me? Do I sound like him?"

Ajax took off his dress shirt and set it on top of his jacket. "No. There's a subtle difference between confident and conceited. You're sure of your worth. He's positive there's no one he can't push to their knees. You're perfect."

With each word, Lucas' expression turned more heated by the second. The laughter died, replaced by desire. "You look like a man with a purpose."

Ajax didn't respond. He took off his undershirt. His hands dropped to his belt.

Lucas' stare burrowed into him. His gaze followed Ajax's hands as he slipped his belt from the belt loops and tossed it in the direction of his shirts. Without a word, he lifted Lucas' blankets and climbed beneath them. He didn't stop until his body covered Lucas and their mouths met. It was time he reserved his spot at the front of the line. Kash couldn't have Lucas. Lucas belonged with Ajax.

Lucas had no clue what went on inside Ajax's head, but whoa. He was intense today, and Lucas wanted that passion on his dick. It had been way too long since Lucas fucked anyone. No matter how weak he felt, his mind and body still craved sex. Lucas' thin pajama pants did nothing to hide how hard he was. Thankfully, Ajax's thin dress pants also didn't hide a thing. Ajax wanted him too, and it was an ego stroke he desperately needed. Lucas knew he looked like shit right now. He had been tall and lanky before the attack. Now he was nothing but sharp bones and disgusting scars.

Ajax's hand ran down his body and found its way beneath Lucas. He squeezed Lucas's ass and used the motion to rock against him. The friction made Lucas a little dizzy. Ajax kissed a path to Lucas' neck.

With Lucas' mouth free, he couldn't stay quiet. He was too aroused. "I can't even think right now. You've stolen every ounce of blood from me. It's throbbing in my dick. I want to be inside you. Let me in. I want to fuck you."

Ajax kissed his way back to Lucas' mouth, responding between kisses. "You will. Just not today. You're not ready."

Lucas legitimately thought he might cry. He was painfully erect, and Ajax kept teasing him. "Have you been ordered to torture me?"

Ajax pulled away just enough to hold Lucas' stare. "This is one place no one is allowed to order me to do anything. No one dictates what happens between you and me but us. I won't have you re-damaging anything because I want you." He swiped his lips across Lucas' mouth. "Don't worry. I still plan to make you blow. All you have to do is enjoy. Plus, that very first kiss fascinated me.

I want more. This isn't about getting instant release. I want to touch you."

Well, fuck. Lucas couldn't argue with that. "Then why are you still talking?"

Ajax's wicked-sounding chuckle vibrated against his skin as he reclaimed Lucas' lips. Now that Lucas knew this wasn't some twisted trick, he was totally in. He savored every swipe of Ajax's tongue. His hands massaged every inch of Ajax he could reach. Even Ajax's hair got Lucas' personal treatment. He pulled and tugged, forcing Ajax to bend to the kisses Lucas wanted. Then Lucas slowed down and rubbed Ajax's scalp in apology for the rough treatment. The moans coming from Ajax led him. Penetration or not, Lucas needed Ajax to walk away from this, knowing Lucas could and would ruin him for everyone else.

Ajax's hips rolled. The friction between them was back. This time, Ajax didn't stop. He rode Lucas' body, ensuring they got equal pleasure. Lucas had never been one of those people who made out and then walked away. He had definitely never blown in his clothes. It looked very much like that was exactly what would happen today. Lucas was oddly okay with this innocent approach. He savored doing something he never had before with someone who mattered in a way no one else had. The closer Lucas got to the edge, the hotter their kiss became. Their actions equally turned desperate. They scratched and squeezed, fighting toward the same goal. Their kiss was needy as hell. They licked and sucked while moaning and gasping. The creep of pleasure climbing his cock had Lucas' muscles clenching. He stopped breathing. Every ounce of focus turned to the pressure beating at his crown. Then the air he held in his lungs burst from him in a gasp before a cry tore from his throat. Ecstasy pulsed through him, taking total control of his brain. The sounds he made were drowned by the sexy as fuck noises coming from Ajax. Lucas was torn between savoring the way his body hummed and drowning in the sight of Ajax as he came. Lucas swore Ajax in the throes of passion was the sexiest thing he had ever seen. Ajax had shown his hand now. Lucas liked what he saw, and he intended to take every advantage.

CHAPTER FIVE

IT HAD BEEN MONTHS since Lucas had a shower that didn't involve nurses. It was nice having Ajax steady against his back while he washed Lucas' body. Every time Lucas thought about Ajax coming in his pants, knowing he had no other clothes there, Lucas bit back a chuckle. Between the two of them, they'd made quite a mess. No one liked wearing cum-soaked clothes. A shower together had sounded so nice. Now Lucas could barely breathe in Ajax's arms. Part of it was due to standing too long. He really hated this. Lucas was so tired of being tired. Organs just didn't like to get cut to pieces. They bitched when they had scar tissue and less function. He was fucking miserable.

"I'm exhausted with being angry, and weak, and angry at being weak." Lucas didn't know why the confession popped out. Maybe being held while not having to look into Ajax's eyes did something to him. Set his tongue free.

Ajax held him tighter. "I know you're sick of hearing this, but you died. What you went through has a near zero chance of survival, but you made it." Ajax kissed his shoulder. His lips lingered there. When he spoke again, his voice came out softer. "It would've killed me if I lost you."

Lucas closed his eyes and savored the moment. He clung to the sound of Ajax's voice.

"I know I'm just some old bloke who shouldn't be touching you right now. Equally, I'm fully aware you'll pretend this never happened when you're fully back on your feet. That's okay, though. I want you back to tip-top health more than I want my happiness. So, for now, just use my strength. That's all I have to offer. I'll do whatever it takes to help you get better. Just give me time to help you."

Lucas felt entirely too much. There was a reason Lucas had always teased and flirted every time he saw Ajax over the years. Not only did he feel closer and happier with Ajax, but he genuinely wanted him. Not just for sex. He had always been Lucas' secret fantasy. Ajax was one of the biggest things he had always craved for himself and knew he would never have. Yet Ajax held him and confessed to feeling the same. Life definitely had a sense of humor, except Lucas wasn't laughing. He couldn't let Ajax think he went unnoticed.

"You've never been just some old bloke. This nightmare has only had two positive points. My mom has been freer and more cared for since this happened, and then there's you. If this horrible thing never happened, I probably wouldn't have ever moved on you. That has nothing to do with your age, and everything to do with being scared shitless at the thought of losing my best friend." Lucas swallowed. If he didn't say everything right now, he probably never would. "I can live without sex, but I'm not so sure I can live without the way you make me smile."

Ajax smiled against Lucas' neck, where he kept his lips pressed. "Ah. Well. If you didn't act like a right cunt to almost everyone you meet, you wouldn't be stuck with me. You'd still be swimming in dick, but no one cares if you're mean to them if the sex is good enough. Not that I'm complaining. I want you all to myself."

Lucas smiled so big, his face hurt. The entire conversation was so typical of them. Serious but so unserious at the same time. "What are you saying? Are you slipping drugs in my food to keep me down?"

He felt Ajax chuckle more than he heard him. "Nah. Tying you to the bed is more my style. Hopefully, it won't come to that."

Lucas laughed. "Bondage play. Yes!"

He practically felt Ajax's happiness vibrating around him. Suddenly, Ajax turned off the water. "I have a great idea." Ajax turned into a wild man. He grabbed towels and dried Lucas before wrapping a towel around his own waist. Then he led Lucas back to bed. "Sit. Don't move. Give me just a second." Ajax headed for the door. He strolled out without looking to see if anyone was in the hall.

Lucas bit his bottom lip. While it was true Ajax's room was pretty much across from him, the idea of Ajax proudly strolling from Lucas' room in only a towel had him fighting all the smiles. While he hadn't been insulted at all when Ajax had rolled from the bed to hide, he still loved the thought of Ajax not being ashamed of him. This not caring if anyone knew fed his ego, especially since there was a clear difference between yesterday and today. Yesterday, Ajax was on duty, assigned to stay with him all day. Tonight, Ajax was off duty. He had chosen to be with Lucas.

Ajax reappeared, still wearing a towel and holding a bundle of clothes. He was all smiles. "Okay. Let's get dressed so I can take you out for a night on the town. We have your wheelchair. Let's go eat and shop or whatever you want to do."

Lucas hated pointing out the obvious, but Ajax hadn't known Lucas didn't have a phone. He doubted Ajax knew anything about his finances. "As much as it pains me to say it, I've been stuck in bed for months without working, and with my bills on autopay. My accounts are probably in the negative by now."

Ajax's face screwed up in confusion. "Your accounts aren't in the negative. Noir has been paying your bills and has continued paying your salary. Not to mention, this is a date. I'm taking you on a date," Ajax emphasized the last word, like he needed Lucas to have no misunderstandings. "I'm paying. You're getting spoiled."

Lucas didn't know what to say. Every word blew Lucas' mind. Obviously, he hadn't known about the money situation. But Ajax wanted this to be a date—like they were more than friends. His mind was blown, but the smile stretching his lips told his real feelings. He wanted this. "Okay."

If he wasn't mistaken, Ajax looked relieved, as if he thought Lucas would say no. "Good. Let's do this."

Lucas had no idea where all this was headed. He had thought they were best friends who decided to add benefits. This was better, though. In fact, oddly enough, nothing had ever made him happier.

Lucas looked happier than Ajax could recall. The first few minutes of their outing had been rocky. It was obvious Lucas didn't like being seen in a wheelchair. After a bit, Ajax watched Lucas' shoulders relax. They had gone to several stores. It seemed once Lucas realized Ajax was truly having a good time with him, Lucas loosened up. Ajax practically saw the tension drain from Lucas. He still couldn't believe not only had Lucas simply accepted he no longer had a phone, but he had also thought he had lost everything and hadn't said a word about either. Lucas was definitely one of those people who refused to complain or show an ounce of weakness. Of course, it was likely Lucas had spent his life feeling like he couldn't complain without looking like a bad son.

Ajax couldn't stop staring at Lucas while Lucas eyed the menu he held. He couldn't take it. "I'm sorry."

Lucas' chin lifted. His eyes were full of life. That was what addicted Ajax in the first place. "Why?" Laughter filled the question, proving Lucas honestly had no idea why Ajax apologized.

"For not doing this earlier." He knew that wasn't enough. "My only excuse is no one has ever scared me the way you did. I mean, as far as dying goes. It's like I've been stuck in overprotective mode. There aren't many people I care about at all. You're on that list, and I'm still trying to recover right alongside you."

Lucas' contagious smile made its appearance. "Don't lie. You just like me better in bed."

Ajax shook his head. There were times he wished Lucas could let his guard down for just a moment. He should have known better than to bother apologizing. Ajax never knew what Lucas actually took to heart. Maybe nothing. It was possible Lucas would never let anyone in. Maybe Ajax should stop trying and just enjoy Lucas' body. Ajax stared at the menu, seeing nothing. He wasn't unhappy. Ajax needed to let it go before he undermined himself.

"Hey."

Ajax's chin lifted. His breath caught. He swore he stared at Lucas' heart.

"Thank you." Lucas didn't make him ask for what. "I know you're one of the biggest reasons I'm alive. You've taken care of me. No one else would've stuck by me the way you have. Other than my mom, obviously, but you know what I mean. I've always known I'll go out badly. But you know what my last thought was that night?" Again, Lucas didn't wait for Ajax to answer. "I thought, at least I was with you."

Ajax had never had such an immediate reaction. His throat swelled nearly closed. No one knew how badly Ajax didn't want this life for Lucas. There was no time better to start the conversation he had been putting off. "I want you to stay." The words tumbled out. Lucas looked every bit as confused as he should.

Ajax started over. "Noir has wanted me to talk to you about making your move permanent for a while now. Your mum is settled in and seems very happy with her newfound freedom and all the extra help. Not to mention, she has people to keep her company. Noir and Lazarus have become very attached to her, and they feel you deserve to be taken care of after everything that's happened."

Lucas blinked a few times before finding his words. "Go back to your original statement."

Ajax took a breath. He had already started this. Ajax was no coward, nor did he feel much of anything for anyone. Lucas was different. "I like having you around. I'd like you to stay."

He could see Lucas struggling to decide whether he should crack a joke or take this seriously. Lucas kept smiling. Then it would disappear just as quickly. Ajax could practically hear Lucas' brain re-booting. An uncertain-sounding chuckle escaped Lucas. "Mom and I already have a place to live."

Ajax felt zero remorse for how he cornered Lucas. "I'm sorry, but no. When Noir's accountant took over your finances, he let your apartment go. The management company said you violated your lease by leaving the flat empty for an extended time." He had another thought. Ajax didn't want Lucas to come unglued. "Don't worry. It was a legal dissolution, and your car is safely tucked away in the garage. The rest of your belongings are stored in the east wing."

"Are you two ready to order?"

Another uncomfortable-sounding chuckle rumbled from Lucas. "I think we need another minute." The moment the server walked away, Lucas jumped in. "Has it occurred to any of you to talk to me about anything? Did you think I wouldn't worry about the entire life I had before this?" He motioned toward the wheelchair. "It feels a hell of a lot like there isn't a single goddamn one of you who thinks I'm a real person with real feelings and responsibilities that don't include you."

Ajax dipped his chin. "You're right to be miffed. I should've spent less time trying to just be with you and more time on what you need besides healthcare. My actions are indefensible and unrealistic. My life has always been very different from yours."

Lucas' smile returned. "You mean, you're used to everything paying for itself without limit."

Some tension left Ajax's shoulders, making him realize how stiff he had become. He had braced for the blow of Lucas leaving him. "I suppose you're right."

They held each other's stare. Heat built between them the way it always did.

"I'll talk to Mom and think about it."

Ajax dipped his chin, acknowledging his decision. "That's all I can ask."

Lucas smirked. "Is it?"

Damn. Sometimes Ajax felt his age. He wondered what went through Lucas' mind when he looked at Ajax the way he did now. Did he really crave Ajax as much as his expression claimed? Or maybe Ajax was just the closest dick.

Still, Ajax was willing to play. "Is there something else you want me to ask for?"

Lucas' wicked expression didn't budge. "No need. You have my full permission to do anything you want to me... with me. Either way, really."

"I'll hold you to that."

The server reappeared while they held each other's stare. Promise flowed between them. When Lucas looked away to place his order, Ajax had to take a breath. Half dead or not, Lucas hadn't lost an ounce of sexual allure. One day soon,

Ajax would sit on Lucas' dick. That day couldn't get here soon enough.

CHAPTER SIX

IT SEEMED AS IF work kept Ajax away more often than not. Lucas wasn't dumb. They had ruined their friendship. He had known that before he had stolen that first kiss. That was what Lucas did, though. He was incapable of holding on to friends. His personality always moved things to the bedroom and then he had no one. Lucas had no clue why he was this way. He knew he was incapable of being real with anyone. In this case, Lucas had been realer than he had ever been. It seemed he was no catch either way. So, really, it was best he kept his heart out of the mix.

The good thing about Ajax not being around as often, Lucas had been forced to do more on his own. Every day, he got stronger and more independent. He had gone from pushing himself around in his wheelchair to moving about the house with his walker. It had only been two weeks since he had gone to dinner with Ajax. But every day that Ajax had an excuse not to stay with him, Lucas' determination to leave grew stronger. He hadn't given Noir an answer about staying. Lucas' mind had turned against him, deepening the depression he always kept hidden. The blacker his thoughts turned, the more self-destructive he became. It was time for Lucas to speak with his mom.

Carrying himself with as much swagger as he could with a walker, Lucas cut into her lunch with the family. After all, it seemed Noir and his bunch were her family now. Lucas needed to put her happiness first. Lucas ignored Ajax's stare. In fact, Lucas didn't look at anyone except his mom.

"Can I steal you away?"

Wendy was all smiles. She always was. "Of course, baby." Wendy cast a look around. "Please excuse me."

She pushed herself to her feet with her walker. Lazarus shot to his feet to help. Lucas doubled his efforts not to see anyone there.

He led the way of their walker brigade, making his way to her bedroom. Lucas wanted to be out of earshot and somewhere no one could easily eavesdrop. He didn't say a word until they were settled in her private sitting room. It hurt his heart, but his mom deserved the life Noir gave her.

By the time they sat, Wendy looked worried. "Is everything okay?"

Lucas flashed her a smile. She didn't need any stress. Her heart was already bad. "Everything is fine. I just wanted to talk to you. We haven't had much of a chance lately."

Guilt passed over Wendy's features. "I'm sorry. I guess I've really taken advantage of some newfound freedom. You know I'd never knowingly ignore you."

Lucas shook his head. "I don't feel ignored. Don't worry about that. You have no idea how happy I am watching you get to do all the things you've been robbed of doing for years. This is the life you deserve. In fact, that's kind of what I wanted to talk to you about. Ajax asked, on behalf of Noir, that we stay. I think you should."

Confusion etched her features. They looked so much alike. She might be his mom, but Wendy had also always been his person. His closest friend and the only normalcy he had. Lucas needed her to be happy, even if it hurt him.

"Why do you say it like that? You want me to stay, but you don't intend to stay with me?"

Lucas swallowed past the lump growing in his throat. "Yes. You've grown really close to Noir and Lazarus." They would keep her safe in a way Lucas couldn't. "With all the extra help here, you have your life back. I want that for you, but once I'm fully on my feet, there's no reason for me to stay."

Her spine stiffened and Lucas bit back a groan. "Absolutely not. We stick together. I don't need any of this as much as I need my son. Noir asked me a few weeks ago to stay. I told him then that the decision would be yours to make. It's always been the two of us."

A sad smile tugged at the corners of Lucas' mouth. "We'll still see each other." He hoped. Maybe Lucas would start over somewhere new. "Seriously, you should stay."

Her eyes filled with tears. Wendy's voice shook when she spoke. "No. I go where you go."

Frustration welled inside Lucas. Of course, he wanted to be the one who took care of her, but that also meant doing what was best for her. This place was what was best. "I just want you to be happy."

"I'm happiest with my son."

Lucas' shoulders fell. He would have to run and hope she understood. "Okay. We'll stay here. You're happy here and I want you to enjoy life. That's a lot more possible with Noir's people."

She didn't look relieved. "Are you sure we should stay? That feels an awful lot like becoming a burden. We've already probably stayed well past our welcome."

Lucas faked a bright smile. He could do this for her. "Noir's the one who asked. It seems they've fallen in love with you and want you here." He saw the hope in his mom's eyes. His heart broke a little. He had always thought he would take care of her to the end, but he had to do what was right. She loved it here and was safe. When Lucas ran, he wouldn't likely see her again.

"I mean, if you're sure. I think this will be great for you too. You can have a life without me weighing you down. I've always wanted you to get to act your age. If we stay here, you can. You could actually date someone for real."

A genuine smile snapped to Lucas' lips. Only his mom would think anyone would want him for real. "Sure, Mom."

The darkness inside him got blacker and swallowed him a little more by the second. He listened to his mom chatter happily about how much she loved it here and how happy going places again made her. Lucas hated himself for all the things he had never been able to do for her. In another week or so, he would be strong enough to disappear. He would miss everything about her. At least someone would love her the way she deserved.

Lucas hadn't even looked at him. Ajax couldn't take it. He had tried giving Lucas time and space. Ajax hadn't wanted to pressure Lucas or take advantage of his vulnerable state. After their amazing day together, it had occurred to Ajax that maybe everything between them was truly a case of Ajax being convenient. Ajax had gotten inside his own head and undermined everything. He wanted Lucas to choose to stay because he wanted to be here. From what he saw from Lucas today, Ajax had done the wrong thing. Not only had Lucas looked hurt, but Ajax was pretty damn certain he wouldn't see Lucas again once he regained his strength.

Ajax chewed his bottom lip and stared at the doorway where Lucas had disappeared with his mom. If only Lucas would come back and look at him. Surely, he would see the way Ajax felt too much. They had been best mates for years. Ajax hadn't wanted to crave Lucas' body for every second of that time, but he had. Now they had crossed a line Ajax couldn't uncross, and he scared the hell out of himself. This was exactly why he had stayed quiet and forced himself to joke about Lucas' bed hopping. Ajax had known he would lose his friend. He had known he wouldn't be special. Ajax wasn't ready for that outcome.

Wendy reappeared without Lucas. Ajax's heart dropped even farther. She looked worried. Wendy smiled the same, but there was something in her eyes.

She reclaimed her seat and cleared her throat. "I hate living at everyone else's mercy. That's why I haven't answered anyone about staying here." Her cheeks turned red, and Ajax's heart twisted. He couldn't imagine what it must be like to be totally dependent on other people to survive. "Anyhow, Lucas says you've talked to him, and since he wants what's best for me, we'll stay."

Lazarus jumped in. "You've brightened our lives since you came to live with us. We love having you here."

A deep, worried-looking line appeared between Wendy's eyebrows. "What about Lucas? I have to think of him too. My heart is so warm knowing you two care about me as much as I care about you, but I don't want to stay and have my son to feel like he's just baggage when, really, I've always been his burden."

Noir made a dismissive gesture. "Don't worry over that. Neither of you is anyone's baggage. You've become like a second mother to us, but Lucas is equally wanted here. The boy almost died helping me." Ajax bit back a snort at Noir calling Lucas a boy when Lucas was older than him. Being a prince was a different life, though. Noir had never been a child. He probably felt ancient.

Noir kept going. "Besides, Lucas is Ajax's closest friend. Ajax doesn't really work the sort of job that allows him to make many of those. He would very much enjoy having Lucas around."

Every word of that kind of made Ajax want to punch Noir. Instead, he flashed Wendy a kind smile.

She glanced between them. "Okay."

It was like the room held its breath. Lazarus broke first. "Was that an okay you'll stay?"

Her hands lifted and fell. "Yes." She still sounded unsure, but that obviously didn't matter to anyone. Lazarus hugged Wendy.

Noir looked his way, wearing the same bored expression he always wore. "You should return to your duties with Lucas."

Ajax dipped his chin and stood. He measured his steps on his way to Lucas' room. After their dinner, he had gone back to his job of sticking to Noir. No one had questioned the move, since guarding Noir had been his entire life. It was his job. Returning to his position had been an easy excuse to give Lucas space. Now he couldn't get back to Lucas quickly enough. Lucas needed to look at him. He had to tell Ajax to his face he didn't want him. He wouldn't take losing his friend lying down. In fact, Ajax might have stormed Lucas' room a little too intensely. He found Lucas thrown across the bed and passed out. The fight went out of Ajax. He closed the door behind him softly and crossed the room. Lucas had been pushing himself too hard, no doubt trying to leave Ajax behind.

Ajax stooped and gently moved Lucas' hair out of his eyes. Damn. He was breathtaking. All the lost weight had made his face sharper. Ajax swore nothing made Lucas less. He had a sexiness that came from the inside. It bled through his pores and overwhelmed anyone within flirting distance. Ajax had never been immune. Ajax stood and stripped down to his underwear. He closed all the curtains and locked the door. Lucas never budged. Ajax rearranged his body so he could cover Lucas and climb into bed bedside him. Lucas needed rest. Ajax would stay right here and make damn sure he got it.

CHAPTER SEVEN

THE SENSATION OF A hot mouth sucking his neck pulled Lucas from his sleep. With his eyes closed, Lucas savored Ajax's scent and the way his body hummed with Ajax's tongue on him. His fingers found Ajax's thick locks and held on, stopping Ajax from moving away. A low moan vibrated from his throat and reality slowly sank in. That had Lucas pushing Ajax away.

"Whoa. You can't get your rocks off and then ignore me for two weeks until you're horny again. There're people I'd let get away with that, but you're not one of them. You're supposed to be my friend." Even Lucas knew he sounded like a clingy crush who never took a hint. Lucas hated that.

Ajax settled in on top of Lucas, ensuring he couldn't get away. His sexy steel-colored eyes held his stare. "I was trying to give you space and time to think. You've been trapped here. I don't want this to be like some weird kind of Stockholm syndrome. I need you to want me because you actually desire to be with me. Unfortunately, it looks as if I've given you too much space. Or I was right to be concerned. You don't sound like a man who wants me."

While holding Ajax's stare, Lucas pushed Ajax's underwear down one hip. He refused to look away as he did the same to the other side. "Do I look like a man who doesn't crave every inch of you?"

Ajax's eyes looked unfocused. Lucas wasn't sure Ajax saw anything at all. It was as if he had turned inside himself, savoring Lucas's hands on his body. Nothing could have told Lucas how badly Ajax truly wanted him than his expression. Some reactions couldn't be faked. The way Ajax was hard for him and lost in desperation was real. That shit could get addictive. Lucas' ego needed this. Maybe his heart did too.

"I hope you didn't start this unprepared. You know I'm in no position to protect you or ease the ride." He loved being blunt with Ajax. When it came to Ajax,

Lucas always found himself acting dirtier than he had ever done with anyone. It was the royal polish. Lucas wanted Ajax down in the dirt with him. He craved seeing the posh veneer vanish.

Ajax grabbed his jaw and bit Lucas' bottom lip before pulling away to hold his stare. He looked exactly like a man bent on rocking Lucas' world. "Don't worry about me, luv. I'm the king of bead lube. Some things come with age." He reached beneath the blankets and came out with a condom. "I think I should show you."

Damn. It had been way too long since he had been inside anyone. Ajax might actually be the one who ruined Lucas for all others while walking away, totally disappointed.

That didn't mean Lucas was finished talking shit. "I think it's time for you to sit on my dick and prove it."

Ajax climbed from the bed and stripped off his underwear. He had a gorgeous body. Cut muscles from years of protecting a prince, being the strongest soldier, made Ajax a vision to behold. The way he looked at Lucas—like he planned to do all the bad things to him—was hot as hell. Lucas was ready to blow inside his briefs.

While Lucas gripped the headboard like it was his last wisp of sanity, Ajax peeled off the remainder of Lucas' clothes. As he dragged Lucas' underwear down his legs, Ajax bent and licked the pre-cum from Lucas' crown. Lucas fought not to lift his hips and chase Ajax's mouth. Heat flashed in Ajax's eyes as he rolled the condom down Lucas' erection. Lucas couldn't focus on anything beyond Ajax's intensity. By the time Ajax straddled his hips again, Lucas had blocked out the entire world. Ajax had his full attention. Lucas was spellbound. He couldn't look away from the sight of every muscle moving in Ajax's torso as he took Lucas' cock.

The breath stuttered from Lucas' lungs. "That's it, beautiful. Take what you want." Lucas couldn't let go of the headboard. All he could do was lift his hips in time with Ajax's movements. Then Lucas made a fatal mistake. He met Ajax's stare. Real feelings stared back at him. Over the past few years, their friendship had slowly grown into something else. Lucas saw everything he felt reflected back at him. The mood in the room changed. Lucas let go of the headboard. He had to touch Ajax. A newfound energy burst through him. He rolled upward, snagged Ajax's waist and easily flipped, tucking Ajax beneath him. Every hint of weakness disappeared. Lucas snagged the top of the headboard, leaving Ajax to hold his legs while Lucas got his core workout. With his free hand, he held Ajax's jaw, keeping Ajax from looking away. He felt the intensity rolling off him. Lucas could and would addict Ajax to his touch. The flush on Ajax's cheeks and the way he gasped for air were like heroin to Lucas. He couldn't look anywhere else. He needed to burn every second into his brain. Lucas felt Ajax tense. The temptation to give in to the pleasure and blow was crippling. Instead, he changed positions, purposely stopping Ajax from coming. He claimed Ajax's mouth, pillaging. Lucas tore his mouth away as a tingle hit at the base of his spine. His balls drew up tight. Lucas ruthlessly changed angles and speed, denying himself an orgasm.

Ajax made a sexy sound that proved Lucas hit at the perfect angle.

Lucas pressed his lips against Ajax's ear. He let his hot breath brush the shell, bringing chill bumps to Ajax's skin. He felt them rise. Lucas thrust hard. "Who owns this body?" The growled question fell from him without a single thought. He was too far gone. Ajax felt too good on his dick. He felt right. Ajax was every bit as perfect as Lucas had always known he would be.

Ajax moaned.

Lucas thrust harder and faster. He had to know how Ajax looked when he blew. "Answer me." Lucas' demand sounded deadly—more like he intended to kill him than show him pleasure. "Who owns this body?"

"You."

The raspy and shaky-sounding reply was all it took. Lucas' entire body stiffened before jerking so hard, he thought he might have actually had a seizure.

Ajax cried out beneath him and his asshole twitched, bringing a second wave of ecstasy scorching through him. The sounds Ajax made had the wildest thoughts running through Lucas' mind at a time he shouldn't be able to think. What if Lucas was the one whose soul had been stolen? What if no one else was ever good enough again? Was it possible he had fallen in love with Ajax over the years? Lucas needed to know.

Nothing about Lucas was merely a boast. Every whispered story about how he was a ride everyone needed to try hadn't been exaggerated. Lucas had been completely focused and crazily intense. Ajax had never experienced a harder orgasm in his life. It was as if Lucas knew exactly how to build a man into a frenzy before setting him free. Ajax still hadn't recovered. It was like he was in a state of shock.

Lucas hadn't gone back to sleep—the way Ajax had expected and usually got from other men. He kept kissing Ajax like he was precious. His head was fully fucked with. Being pressed against Lucas had gotten the best of him. He hadn't been able to stop himself from waking Lucas, so he could touch him the way he wanted. Why had things been so perfect? There was no going back.

With his eyes closed, Ajax savored Lucas kissing and sucking his neck. His body practically vibrated with happiness and contentment.

"You taste amazing. I can't stop."

Butterflies stirred in Ajax's gut. His mouth ran without his brain. "I've missed you. It's been hard as hell trying to give you space. I hated every second."

He felt Lucas smile against his skin. "Yeah. Let's not do that again."

Ajax ran his hands down Lucas' back until he cupped Lucas' ass. "You have nothing to worry about. I might act a right berk at times, but I never make the same mistake twice."

Lucas lifted his head. His eyes swam with humor. "What in the hell is a berk?"

"An idiot. I was a fucking idiot."

Lucas' smile grew. "Well, luckily for you, I find that hot. But maybe don't pull that shit again."

A bark of laughter burst from Ajax. "No worries. You might want to demand the opposite. I might never leave this bed again."

Lucas' expression turned serious. He stroked Ajax's jawline with his knuckles. "I guess that means I have to stay."

The massive wave of longing that washed over Ajax scared the hell out of him. He was really in trouble. "I'd love that." Even

Ajax heard the honesty in his voice. He stopped himself before he offered Lucas the world. Unfortunately, he couldn't fully control his tongue. "You should probably move to my room, though. That way, you could have your own kitchen and all that."

Lucas' gaze moved over Ajax's face. "Everyone will know about us."

Ajax shrugged. "As long as you're saying there is an us, nothing would make me happier than everyone knowing you're mine."

Lucas' intensity didn't waver. His hand ran down Ajax's side. "I already told you, you're mine. Never think anything I say when I'm inside you is heat-of-the-moment shit. I'm always in control."

A shiver ran through Ajax. He had a feeling he should take that as a threat. Ajax wanted more of this all-consuming ferocity. He was invested.

"Kiss me again."

Lucas' piercing stare never softened as he lowered his head, giving Ajax what he wanted. Ajax would have to let Lucas go back to sleep. He needed his strength. Plus, it was the middle of the night. But for a few more minutes, Ajax's heart demanded attention. It was possible Ajax had fallen at some point over the years. Lucas wasn't known for sticking around. That was fine. Ajax had known he would grow old alone. His position with the royal family meant his first responsibility would always be to the crown. He couldn't expect anyone to understand that. For him, there were much worse things than a life of service. He had already lived that life. Ajax would never go back again.

CHAPTER EIGHT

LUCAS: *I SAW YOU training with your men this morning. That's hot.*

Ajax: *I have to keep them sharp.*

Lucas: *When you're finished, you should definitely bring that sweaty ass to me. I have plans for it.*

Ajax: *I'll see you in five minutes.*

Ajax: *How much longer will you be gone?*

Lucas: *Probably thirty to forty-five minutes. Why? Do you need anything?*

Ajax: *No. I just wanted to know when I should start worrying.*

Lucas*: LOL! I'm a big boy.*

Ajax: *Trust me. I know.*

All it took after moving to Ajax's room was one month. Lucas had graduated to a cane. With his hands gripping the wheel, Lucas savored driving around town. It was a taste of freedom Lucas had wondered if he would ever experience again. He took full advantage. Lucas took more turns around town than necessary before finally heading for his destination. When he pulled into the driveway of Dr. Kace and Jamison Brightly's house, he took a calming breath. It wasn't like Lucas to be nervous. Truly, he wasn't. He couldn't describe how he felt. Kace had saved his life. That same doctor had married Lucas' ex—the only one Lucas had actually cared about. Of course, like most everything in his life, Lucas had screwed that up. Funnily enough, he had also had sex with Kace. It seemed he brought people together. Not that any of that shit mattered any longer. He had Ajax.

Just thinking Ajax's name made Lucas smile as he used his cane to struggle from the car while hanging on to his reason for being there. It took a lot longer to make it to the door than he cared to admit. He also had to do some shuffling to ring the doorbell. Thankfully, he didn't have to do so twice.

Kace answered. He looked more than a little surprised to see Lucas, but his light green eyes were still lit with happiness. "Wow! Lucas. You're upright and getting around."

His smile brightened everything. Fuck. He was beautiful. There had been a time when Lucas regretted not trying harder to win Kace's heart. He supposed everything worked out for the best.

Lucas laughed. "Barely."

Jamison appeared behind Kace. He was just as big and cuddly-looking as Lucas remembered. He smiled like he was genuinely happy to see Lucas. That was a mind fuck. "Hey. I thought I heard your voice. Come in."

Lucas waved off the offer. "Thank you, but no. I've already been out and about longer today than I should've been. My battery is starting to fail. I just wanted to stop by to thank you both for saving my life. Since I don't actually know what you give someone who doesn't let you die when they probably should have, I brought flowers." He passed them to Kace. It felt like such a lame gift now that he was here. He shifted from foot to foot. Lucas hadn't realized how uneasy he would be until it happened. All the high emotions he had been riding since waking up were new. They were uncomfortable.

"These are gorgeous. Thank you." Kace sounded like he meant it. "You didn't have to get us anything. It's my job to keep people alive. Seriously, though. You should come in and sit down."

Lucas took a step back. "Nah. I'm good. Like I said, I just wanted to stop by and say thanks. Sorry I didn't stop by sooner, but you know." An uncomfortable-sounding chuckle escaped him. "I guess I should go before I fall."

Kace stepped out. Concern etched his features. "Do you need some help getting back to the car?"

As much as Lucas appreciated the offer, it also pricked his pride. Everyone still saw him as weak. He was, but he was also on the mend. "No. Seriously. I'm good. I'll see you around, I guess."

Lucas turned to cane his way down the steps.

Jamison obviously didn't think he could do it. He grabbed Lucas' elbow and helped him stay upright. When Lucas wobbled a little, he was grateful for the help. Still, it chafed to have to thank Jamison again, especially since Lucas wasn't dumb. He knew Jamison hated him.

"Thanks." Lucas sounded more bitter than appreciative. He couldn't help it. Lucas was still a little bitter. Ajax made things worthwhile, but still. Months of his life had been stolen.

Jamison helped him to the car. "How's your mom?"

"Living her best life at Noir's," Lucas answered honestly. Again, he sounded bitter. He was glad she was happy, but sad he couldn't give her what she needed.

Jamison nodded. He didn't look Lucas's way. "I'd heard you two were living there now."

It took everything Lucas possessed not to stop dead and demand where he had heard that. "Yeah. I guess it might be permanent. Mom has a much better quality of life now."

Jamison opened his car door for him. He looked as if he fought not to say something. Apparently, he lost the battle. "Are you sure you two are safe? What will Noir expect in return for this kindness he doesn't possess? It'll probably be a lot more than you can afford to lose."

Oh, Lucas knew. He had thought about that more times than he could count. Lucas climbed into the car and met Jamison's stare. He felt like Jamison had always deserved a huge apology from him. Thanks to dating Lucas, Jamison had been pulled way too deeply into Noir's realm. No one deserved that. "I know you'll never believe it, but I'm genuinely sorry you got dragged into things. No doubt you also won't believe that I didn't have any more of a choice than you did. I'm glad you got out and found a happy life with a great guy. But there's never been any chance I'll be free." Most of the time, Lucas wasn't sure he wanted to be. He was tired. Lucas might be young, but he had been responsible for things someone his age should never have to be responsible for, and he was exhausted. So, no matter what Noir wanted in return, Lucas would do it. But Jamison didn't know everything. He hadn't been as enmeshed as Lucas, so he kept trying to ease Jamison's worries. "I know Noir does terrible shit, but he keeps the town fentanyl free, and he pours a lot of money into local charities. He's not totally heartless. At home, he's just some guy really in love with his husband."

Jamison's face grew harder with every word and didn't soften. "That 'just some guy' would slit your throat and not look back."

Lucas shrugged. "I knew that going in and I still did this to myself. There's no going back."

Jamison's shoulders fell. "Just watch out for yourself. If you ever decide you're done, call me. We'll figure something out."

Lucas flashed a smile he didn't feel. "I will." He absolutely wouldn't. Jamison had a good life now. Lucas wouldn't steal it.

With a sharp nod, Jamison closed his door and headed back toward his waiting husband. A wave of sadness washed over Lucas. When he had been with Jamison, he had secretly believed they would have a great life together. Lucas had dreamed of normalcy and a steady existence. Unfortunately, Lucas was broken. There was something missing from him, a moral compass or genuine sympathy. He didn't know, but he never felt bad for being bad. Lucas was oddly good at running drugs and collecting money. He had a cold side he had never wanted Jamison to see. That had never been an option.

Lucas put the car in reverse and headed home. Home. That felt so odd. At least Lucas knew a good man waited there for him. Ajax knew all Lucas' sides and wanted him exactly as he was. They shared a common wickedness. It was a trait that was absolute fire in bed. While it hurt to think of Jamison and all they could have been, he was happier in this relationship with Ajax than he had ever been. His days and nights with Ajax were like some sort of miracle, eclipsing everything else in his life. Lucas understood where he had been wrong in the past. His life with Ajax was built on friendship. It was a lot like a sleepover with his best friend every night. Lucas hadn't really had that kind of childhood. He had been a huge loner, always finding trouble. Ajax was the kind of trouble Lucas could get into for the rest of his life.

By the time Lucas parked in his spot in the garage, he had regained a bit of energy. Plus, all his thoughts about Ajax had him ready to hunt the guy down. As he pushed his way inside, Lucas carefully toed off his shoes inside the mudroom before stepping into the kitchen.

"Surprise!"

Lucas's heart leaped into his throat. He stood like a statue, blinking at the crowd that filled the room. His mom and Ajax wore matching shit-eating grins. Since Lucas had never done more than share a nice meal with cake afterward with his mom, he hadn't expected anyone else would notice it was his birthday.

"Um. Wow. I don't know what to say."

His mom pushed her walker his way and put a crown on his head. "You don't have to say anything. It's your day. Everyone wants to share it with you."

Lucas was a hell of a lot more moved than he knew how to express. His gaze found Ajax. The truth hit like a truck. He really was in love. They were the real deal. Nothing else mattered anymore.

Lucas looked like they had shocked all the sense from him. He smiled and thanked everyone as they wished him a happy birthday. Their gazes kept meeting before Lucas was torn away again. Lucas' shell-shocked expression never lessened even as he ate cake and opened presents.

Ajax kept a slight distance and let everyone else bombard Lucas. He needed Lucas to see that Ajax wasn't the only one who wanted him here.

Even though Lucas had lived with them for several months, Ajax still saw the sadness in him. He watched Lucas visibly feel separate from everyone else—like he wasn't one of them. More than that, Lucas tried to pretend he didn't feel as if he had lost his only parent to a new family. Lucas just genuinely didn't think anyone cared about him. It had taken Ajax way too long to see that truth. Lucas' humor was a mask, shielding his heart from rejection. Ajax wanted so badly for Lucas to understand this was his place to fall. They were his family.

Way too much time for Ajax's sanity passed before Lucas refused to let Ajax continue steering clear. Lucas' heated expression as he moved Ajax's way had Ajax's feet frozen to the floor. Ajax would give him anything as long as he continued looking at Ajax like he loved him. Fuck, Ajax wanted that.

"You did this, huh?"

Ajax couldn't stop smiling. "Your mom helped."

Lucas shook his head, looking blown away. "I didn't realize you even remembered it was my birthday."

Ajax scoffed before he could stop it from happening. "I have never missed even one of your birthdays." And Lucas had never missed his. Honestly, until that moment, Ajax hadn't noticed exactly how blind they were.

"We're idiots."

A bark of laughter escaped Ajax at Lucas, saying Ajax's thoughts aloud. They were so ridiculously alike. Ajax nodded. "We really are. I know you didn't have a gift from me in that pile. I'd rather give it to you when we're alone."

Laughter flashed in Lucas' eyes. "Yeah, I'll bet."

An exasperated huff burst from Ajax. "I'll have you know it's a real gift, but I can tie a ribbon around myself if you'd like."

The way Lucas' smile never dimmed was addictive. It was like they were completely alone. Everyone ceased to exist. Lucas cast a quick glance around. Before Ajax knew what would happen, Lucas quickly darted into the pantry with Ajax in tow. The moment they were closed away and out of sight, Lucas was in his space. Their lips met, and they shared each other's air. So much emotion rose inside Ajax as their tongues met. He wanted this to be forever. His throat swelled. Ajax hadn't been looking for this. He had no idea where he thought things would go between them when he started down this road, but somewhere along the line, Ajax had...

Lucas dropped to his knees, killing every thought in Ajax's head. He stared down the line of his body, transfixed by the sight of Lucas unzipping his pants. Ajax wanted to say they were feet from their entire family. He knew he should point out they could get busted any second. Lucas would definitely be horrified if his mom caught him blowing Ajax in the middle of his birthday party. No words formed. He was down Lucas' throat so fast, Ajax couldn't truly think at all. Ajax definitely couldn't speak. He bit his tongue to keep from moaning. Damn, Lucas knew how to play his body. That mouth had too much fucking talent. Ajax had really gone into things, thinking he would bend Lucas, addicting him and twisting him around Ajax's finger. Something else had happened. Ajax hadn't been prepared. Lucas sucked and swallowed, getting the quick results he obviously wanted. The pressure built until Ajax's sanity was balanced on the edge of a knife. Then Lucas pulled some move with his tongue that had Ajax catching sight of heaven.

Lucas kissed his way back to Ajax's lips.

While Ajax still tried to catch his breath, and he shook from the powerful orgasm,

Ajax couldn't control himself. His mouth opened, and the truth fell out. "I love you."

Lucas pulled away and held Ajax's stare. His cheeks were flushed, and his lips were swollen. His expression had Ajax ready to ride his dick. He needed that heat beneath him. There was no shock or rejection in Lucas' eyes. It was Ajax who ended up in disbelief when Lucas responded, "I love you too."

Like that, Ajax knew they were forever. He would never let Lucas go.

Chapter Nine

Ajax: I *wish you* *would come with me to these things. You're always invited. Salem and his pretty boys are interesting enough, but I'm not truly a guest at these parties. I'm on duty. It's boring.*

Lucas: *To be fair, you'd still be on duty if I was there.*

Ajax: *True, but I could quietly swap locations and find a dark corner for us.*

Lucas: *I'll be there in ten.*

Lucas: *My legs feel like jelly and my hands are shaking so hard I can barely type.*

Ajax: *You need to stop trying to overdo it at the gym. I know you need to rebuild your full strength, but it won't happen overnight.*

Lucas: *I want to pin you against the wall and fuck you hard—the way you deserve. That won't happen until I'm back to one hundred percent.*

Ajax: *Mhmm. Interested. But it's not worth it to me if it comes at the price of your health. I love you. I need you to take things slow.*

Lucas: *Your desires are my top priority. I love you too. If you want me to slow down, I will. We have all the time in the world, right?*

Ajax: *Right.*

Lucas: *Plus, I'm wasting too much energy. Half dead or not, I'll be inside you tonight. But I realize I won't be at my best. You deserve top-tier service.*

Ajax: *Don't worry. I'll still get it. You can just relax while I take control.*

Lucas: *I can't wait.*

Ajax: *I love you.*

Lucas: *I love you too.*

Ajax: *I hope your passport is up to date. We're expected in Serveno in a little less than a month.*

Lucas: *Oh. All right. Just tell me what to pack.*

Ajax: *The royal tailor will be here on Wednesday. Noir will ensure your mother and you have the proper attire to mingle with royalty.*

Mom: *Did you hear we're going to a royal ball?!! I'm so excited! Lazarus says*

someone is coming to take my measure-ments and discuss colors. I feel just like a princess.

Lucas: *That's great. You'll outshine everyone.*

Mom: *Flatterer.*

Lucas: *Just being honest.*

Mom: *I love you. You have no idea how proud I am of you every day.*

Lucas: *I love you too.*

Lucas: *I'll be waiting with bells on for this tailor.*

Ajax: *You'll be the sexiest man in Serveno. Everyone will be jealous of me.*

Lucas was absolutely certain no one would even notice him in Serveno. At least, he hoped that was true. Logically, Lucas understood he dated the general of Noir's royal guard. A soldier that had risen in the ranks so fast and young, he impressed an entire kingdom and landed the lofty position as Noir's personal guard. Lucas had always been fully aware he lived with an actual prince. It was just easy as hell to forget those things since they lived in America and Noir was just a normal person at home. For the most part. Kind of. He was the typical ridiculously wealthy person who could and would slaughter a person in a heartbeat and immediately get back to his breakfast. All of that aside, Lucas hadn't once considered what it truly meant to live as part of the royal family. He never thought he would meet a king. Lucas definitely never saw himself on the arm of someone as powerful as Ajax. Butterflies stirred in Lucas' stomach. He really got to fuck that anytime he wanted. It was sad how much Lucas wanted to hunt down Ajax and throw him over his shoulder caveman style. Lucas just couldn't seem to get enough. Ajax was a sickness. Lucas desperately wanted to feel this forever.

Lucas lifted his booted foot and set it on the chair. As he tied the black leather combat-style boot, the bedroom door opened. A very pissed-off-looking Ajax strolled into the room. His rage-filled gaze skimmed the room. First, his stare locked in the leather bag, waiting for Lucas on the bed. Then his total fury focused on Lucas.

"I'd hoped Portland had been taking the mickey out when he called, asking for the time and place of your arrival. What in the fuck are you doing? You're *mine*. This shite is done."

While the growl in Ajax's tone was sexy as hell, Lucas had worried about this. He was finally well enough to get back to work, and he needed to do just that. Noir did everything for Lucas' mom and him. Lucas needed to be useful. He couldn't be a charity case.

"Noir asked this of me. Even if I was positive I could say no, I can't. Knowing

Noir's taste and expectations, the clothes from that tailor alone probably cost every bit of a million dollars. That's just a tiny blip of what he's done for Mom and me. It's just a quick trip to meet Portland. I've done it countless times with zero issues. It'll likely take less than half an hour."

"You're not going. Noir can send your little flirty friend, Kash. He'll do anything for a pound."

Lucas cocked his head to one side. A thought occurred to him. "Does Serveno use UK currency? It seems that's something I should know before our trip."

"Yes. Don't change the subject. I forbid you from doing this. I almost lost you once. That's not something I can do twice."

Lucas dropped his foot to the floor. He closed the distance between them, snagging Ajax's waist and hauling his other half against him. "Sexy, please stop. This is Portland we're talking about. While he can be vicious when crossed, it's me. I'm perfectly safe."

Ajax's eyes burned with something Lucas couldn't explain. He was truly scared and hurt that Lucas would do this to him. "Please don't go."

Lucas' chest ached. He knew Ajax would never lower himself to begging, but he had done so for Lucas. This mattered to him.

He took a deep breath and slowly released it. "I've already told Noir I'll do the run. You know I can't take it back."

Ajax pulled out of Lucas' hold, looking like a man ready to tear down every-thing he knew and possessed. "I fucking can. He's not pulling you back into this bullshit. I love Noir like a son, but he's not doing this to me. This is too much to demand of anyone." Ajax snatched up the leather satchel and stormed from the room.

Lucas pinched the spot between his eyes and blew out a sigh. This was way too much drama over a simple drop. Lucas could see Ajax reacting like this if Lucas had been sent to collect on a debt, or to make a point about missed payments not being tolerated. But this drop was a cakewalk.

With an aggravated huff, Lucas went after Ajax. Ajax must have used one hell of an angry long stride. Lucas had only seen

Ajax walk like that once when someone didn't show up for their shift. The guy was gone. Luckily, he caught sight of him as he stepped inside Noir's private sitting room. The guard outside the door held the leather bag, looking bored.

Lucas flashed him a smile as he moved toward the door. He wasn't entirely sure he would be allowed inside. Ajax's yelled voice reached him before Lucas even made it to the doorway.

"How fucking dare you put Lucas in the position of running again?"

Lucas peeked inside the room, hoping like hell his mom wasn't in there. She would have questions he couldn't answer. Thankfully, it was only Noir and Ajax inside.

Noir's response froze Lucas' feet to the floor before he stepped fully into view. "Your part is done, Ajax. The boy fell into line, agreeing to stay and regaining his strength. You no longer have to pretend to be the lovesick fool."

Lucas' entire body seized for half a second before the pain hit him so hard, the blow rocked him on his feet. His pulse pounded in his ears. Each breath he took gave him less oxygen than the last. Hyperventilating loomed. Then the rage hit. He should have known. He fucking should have known.

Lucas took the bag from the guard and stormed off. He already had his wallet, phone, and keys. Lucas could just walk away now. That was exactly what he did. On his deathbed, Lucas had possessed a clearer mind than he had since he kissed

Ajax. He had known when he was on his final breath that Noir never cared about him. Lucas had been fully aware that he was nothing to any of these people. If he had died, they wouldn't have batted a fucking eye. They wouldn't have even thought about him again.

Lucas was in his car and on his way in under a minute. He would do this one drop and hope it was enough for the prince to keep helping his mom. Lucas didn't care about many things in this world. He had let love blind him. The pains in his chest might very well kill him. He wasn't sure he wasn't actually having a heart attack. Lucas had never felt this much pain, and he had been stabbed repeatedly. Noir wanted this job done so goddamn badly that he had fucked with Lucas' head and heart in a way Lucas couldn't handle.

Lucas called the first name that came to mind. His call was answered on the first ring.

"Hello?"

"I want out."

Thankfully, no questions were asked. Lucas might have driven into a tree if there had been a single inquiry. "I'll text you a meeting spot. Come to me. I'll keep you safe."

A weight lifted from Lucas' chest. The lessened pressure didn't help much, but he stayed conscious. He was scared as hell of what he might do when the shock went away. He might kill someone. No matter what happened, Lucas knew one damn thing. They had finally broken him. He was done.

It took way too long for Ajax to deal with Noir. Thankfully, Noir knew him well enough to know when Ajax wouldn't back down. Hell would freeze before he let this nonsense get Lucas killed. Ajax didn't ask for much for himself, but Lucas was his whole heart. Serveno would have to put him to death for desertion. He used to think there wasn't a single damn thing he would choose over his prince. Now he knew for a fact Lucas came first, even if it cost Ajax everything, including his life.

When Ajax left the sitting room, Hektor still stood at his post, except there was no bag. Ajax was confused as hell. He had settled with Noir, saying he would deliver the goods to Portland. He blinked at Hektor's empty hands.

"I gave you a package to hold."

Hektor looked bored, except for his eyes. His eyes were cold. "Yeah. After hearing you're only faking love to keep him here, Lucas took the bag and left."

The absolute horror that struck Ajax nearly buckled his knees. Somehow, his mouth continued working while his heart raced and his mind reeled. "You just gave it to him." He didn't even know what he said.

Hektor shrugged. "He was ordered to deliver it to Portland. Why would I not give it to him?"

Ajax knew Hektor heard everything that went on in Noir's life. He was equally aware Hektor had heard every word of Ajax's argument with Noir. Hektor also knew damn well Ajax wasn't faking a single fucking thing. At least, he thought Hektor knew that. If Hektor questioned his feelings, he couldn't imagine Lucas' thoughts.

Ajax walked away. He had to talk to Lucas. Ajax had to explain. Yes, Noir had ordered him to do whatever it took to keep Lucas here, but Ajax hadn't needed that command. In fact, Noir's demand had played straight into Ajax's hands. Ajax had known he wanted to keep Lucas before that very first kiss. Noir's plan did nothing but stop Ajax from having to ask permission to make Lucas' presence permanent. Goddamn it. Lucas was out there somewhere thinking nothing about them was real. Fuck everything. Lucas wasn't known for being reasonable. He could disappear. He might do anything—like never look back. Ajax had to talk to him before he did anything they would both regret. He rubbed his chest. It felt a hell of a lot like his heart was breaking. If the shoe was on the other foot, Ajax would never touch Lucas again. He was so totally fucked. Lucas and he were completely alike.

Ajax pulled his phone from the inside pocket of his dress jacket. He checked his messages, hoping against hope Lucas had said anything at all. There was nothing. Ajax called Lucas as he headed for their room, praying Lucas had left a note, even though he knew in his heart Lucas would never do that. He listened to the phone ring while searching every inch of their bedroom for a note. Their room. It had taken three months of Lucas sharing Ajax's bed for everything to become theirs. Ajax couldn't see things any other way. He called four times with no answer. He decided to text, hoping Lucas would at least read what he had to say. Halfway through pouring his heart out, Ajax deleted the paragraph. Lucas deserved to look Ajax in the eyes and see the truth. A text wasn't good enough. He opened the app to track Lucas' phone. When Ajax saw the address, he sat. Thankfully, the couch had been there to save him from hitting the floor. Ajax knew that address. Lucas was done.

CHAPTER TEN

THE SPOT WHERE LUCAS had been attacked was a strange but oddly perfect meeting place. After all, Lucas had chosen this spot to collect for a reason. There were zero cameras anywhere for blocks. Nobody saw anything in this area. There wouldn't be a single witness to Lucas' disappearance. No one would ever know who helped him. He doubted they would even suspect. A movement caught Lucas' attention. Kash's sexy, hard body caught

Lucas' eye first before he found Kash's dark blue gaze.

Lucas didn't know where to start. "Thank you for meeting with me."

A cocky smile stretched Kash's lips. Wind ruffled his dark blond hair. "Of course. I'm the one who's told you countless times to call me when this day came. You started working with Noir too young to have gone into things having an out. I don't work for anyone without a disappearing act in my pocket." He wasn't being condescending. Kash was being realistic. Lucas understood that. He didn't have time to pussyfoot around the issue. It wouldn't take Ajax long to realize Lucas was gone. Any man evil enough to pretend to love him for his prince wouldn't hesitate to do whatever it took to get him back underneath Noir's thumb.

Kash didn't seem to need any explanations. He got straight to the point. "My cousin owns a security company out in California. He has locations all over the country and he's always looking for help."

"I could do security work."

Kash shrugged. "I know you can. You'd never encounter half the shit you do in this profession. Keeping someone safe would be a gravy job for you. I've already talked to him and explained the situation. Since he's always planned for me to disappear into his business, I didn't have to say much. But I let him know you could only stick to people who aren't in the public eye or have any chance of crossing Noir's path." He passed a business card Lucas' way. "Here's his information. That number will take you to his personal line. Check your car for AirTags and ditch your phone. Anything they can track has to go before you leave. Just pick up a burner phone. He's expecting your call. Don't hesitate on this."

An SUV squealing to a stop pulled Lucas' gaze toward a nearby parking lot. Royal guard jumped from the vehicle. He turned to wave Kash away before anyone spotted him. Kash was already gone.

Lucas stuffed the card in his pocket before Ajax appeared. His gaze barely skimmed Ajax's face before he had to look away. Lucas couldn't stand the sight of him. Seeing him hurt too much.

"What are you doing here?" The rage-filled words echoed, bouncing from wall to wall in the cluttered alley.

Lucas swallowed the hurt and stared at a spot over Ajax's shoulder. He wondered if he would fall apart. His throat was too tight. Lucas' eyes felt like sandpaper. He hurt so badly, he didn't know how he stayed upright.

Lucas swallowed. "I'm free to go any-where I want. What are you doing here?"

Ajax invaded his space.

Lucas took a step back, putting distance between them. "No." Goddamn it. Even he heard the agony in his voice.

"Look at me."

Lucas couldn't. It was so much worse than a normal heartbreak. Ajax had pre-tended to be his friend. Everything had been a lie. Ajax was all Lucas had in the world beyond his mom. He had lost her too. Lucas had nothing left to take. Like an injured animal, he might do anything.

A small part of him wanted Ajax to hurt every bit as badly as Lucas did. But mostly, Lucas was just empty.

"I need you to listen to me, okay?"

"Why?" Lucas barked the question with all the fury he felt. "I dropped Noir's package. All of you got what you wanted. A mindless soldier doing the grunt work, acting as the face of the guy who'll go down when shit goes sideways. You should've just left me here to die." Lucas snapped his teeth together so hard and fast, he bit his tongue. He needed to bite the damn thing off. Ajax didn't deserve the satisfaction of seeing the fruits of his destruction.

"Why would you say that? It would kill me if anything happened to you. Didn't you hear me earlier? This isn't the life I want for you. I want you exactly as you've been since you moved to our bedroom. You're supposed to be with me. My only goal is to convince you to marry me. I don't want you anywhere near this."

He sounded so sincere, but Ajax had sounded that way all along. He was being the good general, following orders. Everything about him was fake.

Lucas' vision blurred. He blinked like his life depended on it. Lucas would not fucking cry. He hadn't cried when he had taken his final breath. This wouldn't break him either. He fucking refused.

Lucas stiffened his spine and forced himself to meet Ajax's stare. The move nearly took him out. Ajax genuinely looked as devastated as Lucas. It seemed he was a damn good actor. He should be on the big screen. "I know it's an act, so you can stop now. None of you need to worry I'll snitch or anything. All I can ask is for you to keep looking out for Mom. You won't see me again."

Before Lucas saw it coming, his back was against the wall with Ajax flush against him. Ajax held Lucas' hand against his chest. "I know you feel the way this heart only beats for you. For the first time in my life, I have something beautiful that matters way more to me than my sworn duty to the crown. Say the word. We'll disappear together. Just please don't take my heart and leave me behind. There's no fucking way you can look at me and not know how I feel. There was no goddamn act. In fact, Noir spent a couple of months angry with me for not doing whatever it took to convince you to stay. Everything between us is real."

Lucas didn't know if he trusted Ajax's word. He didn't know if he could ever trust anything about him again. "You pretended to be my friend." There was no stopping the way his voice cracked. The realization his best friend had betrayed him was worse than losing a lover. In his heart, they had run so much deeper than sharing a bed.

"No." Ajax's eyes said he spoke the truth. But his eyes had also shown his love, and that wasn't real. Nothing felt real. Ajax didn't give up. "Tell me how to prove my love. Come home with me. Let me fix this. If you want, we can go straight to Noir and he can tell you everything. I spent quite some time screaming at him this morning for daring to claim I was faking my love. In the end, Noir laughed and said he had only been goading me for not doing right by you. He felt I dishonored you by not making this permanent." Ajax's eyes turned more desperate-looking by the moment. "He's right. I should've tied you to me already. The only reason I haven't asked you to spend the rest of your life with me is because I hadn't spoken to Noir about it. I'm not an American. I'm not free. My life belongs to the crown. I owe the queen and king everything. They plucked me from an abusive family to train me to be a warrior. I had the opportunity to build myself into the highest position a guard can hope to achieve. They're owed my life for that, but you own my soul. If you'll keep me, I'll follow you anywhere. Just please don't take away the only love and friendship I have. No one sees me the way you do. You're the only place I'm free."

Lucas had never been more confused. Maybe if he had stayed to hear Ajax's reaction to Noir's words, then he would know what to do. Ajax looked as if he believed every word coming out of his mouth. Lucas felt more torn than he ever had in his life. It would be so easy to simply reach for the man his heart ached to hold. But Lucas didn't know what was real any longer. Maybe he just wanted to believe and take the easy route.

Ajax dipped his chin. His voice came out in a cajoling whisper. "I love you. Please don't leave me." He kissed the corner of Lucas' mouth. Lucas' walls fell a little more. "Please, Lucas. I need you to see me." He kissed the other corner of Lucas' mouth. "You're everything to me. I can't lose you." He pressed a sweet kiss against Lucas' lips. This time, he didn't move away. He held still, obviously waiting for Lucas to make the next move.

Lucas' mind raced. He went over every minute of the day. Ajax had been outraged at the idea of Lucas making that drop. He had screamed at Noir in a way Lucas doubted Noir had ever seen before. Ajax could have lost his life over that. Why would he do that if this was fake?

In the end, it didn't matter. No force on the planet could have stopped Lucas' lips from parting. His entire being—heart, body, and soul—loved Ajax. Lucas didn't know how to stop.

Ajax shook to his core. He fully expected Lucas to come to his senses and knee him in the groin at any second. Instead, Lucas held the two halves of Ajax's jacket in tight fists, as if scared Ajax would disappear. Tears stung the backs of Ajax's eyes as Lucas' tongue lightly stroked his. From the moment he learned Lucas had heard what Noir said, he had died a little more with each passing second. He had always thought he was infallible, unshakeable. Over the last seven months, Lucas had broken something down inside Ajax. Ajax belonged to Lucas. Wherever he went, Ajax would follow.

Ajax couldn't stop pushing. "Tell me you love me." Each word brushed Lucas' lips.

He couldn't pull away enough to speak. Any distance felt like too much for his heart.

Lucas sniffled, making Ajax realize Lucas silently cried. He had thought it was his tears that fell. Ajax forced himself to pull away enough to confirm his thoughts. Lucas never cried. He had been through hell, died, and came back again, completely changed. Not once through the pain, fear, and anger had Lucas shed a single tear. But he cried for Ajax, and Ajax wasn't sure if he was worthy. Noir had told him to do whatever it took to keep Lucas with them. He had used that command to his advantage to steal Lucas' heart. But Lucas had already stolen him a long time ago, so he saw it as fair, but maybe it wasn't. Ajax didn't know.

Lucas swiped Ajax's cheeks. "Don't cry. What will your minions think?"

A watery laugh burst from Ajax. It seemed he cried after all. He had never been this terrified. Even when he had done CPR to keep Lucas' heart going, he hadn't felt this destroyed. At least the CPR had given him a slight feeling of control—like his hands could bring Lucas back to him. This was different. There was nothing Ajax could do to convince Lucas to keep him. Lucas had to choose all on his own. Ajax had a bad feeling he had nothing to offer.

Still, he clung to whatever he could. "Minions?" He chuckled. "Don't let them hear that. They're honorable soldiers for the crown."

Lucas' slight smile faded away. His voice came out barely audible, as if he couldn't get his throat to work. "I don't know what to think. My heart is screaming for me to believe you. I don't know if it can be trusted. You're the first person I've ever loved this much."

Ajax didn't think. He just acted. "Marry me. Let me spend the rest of my life proving we're as real as love gets."

Lucas sniffed.

Ajax practically felt Lucas' walls falling. "Come on. You know you want to. This is your chance to spend the rest of your life cursing me and making sure I never forget today."

"You know that's not who I am. I have better ways to torture you than berating you for the rest of our lives." The heat that lit in Lucas' eyes had Ajax ready to hit the ground in relief. He would stand here and beg for however long it took to wear Lucas down, but any thought that Lucas wouldn't touch him again was too much. Ajax had never needed anything like he needed their life together.

It was Ajax's turn to fight for his voice. "I've never had anything even close to normal before you. Our version of me coming home to you is my oxygen. You'll never regret me."

"We'll see. You haven't married me yet. Maybe you'll be the one full of regrets."

"Never." Ajax claimed Lucas' mouth with all the hunger in his soul. As long as they were together, Ajax's life was as flawless as any existence could be. He would make sure Lucas remembered that every day. Ajax wouldn't fail again.

CHAPTER ELEVEN

ALL LUCAS COULD DO was stare at Ajax as Ajax drove them home in Lucas' car. His stomach still felt shaky, but Ajax had cried. Lucas expected Hell to freeze over as they went on with life. All Lucas wanted was to be back in their space, inside Noir's home, where they could be alone and just work on them. Maybe some things had been left unsaid. Lucas didn't know. All he knew was they had to stick together while they figured things out.

The card Kash had given him still burned a hole in Lucas' pocket. That new life was still an option. Lucas wasn't as helpless now. He wasn't trapped in this life with no way out. Maybe that mattered more than Lucas had wanted to admit.

"Why that alley?"

Lucas was so lost in enjoying the sight of Ajax. The question startled him. "What?"

Ajax still didn't look his way. "That alley. Why is that where you went?"

As much as Lucas hated to lie, in this case, he had no other choice. "Maybe I just needed to come to terms with some things."

He watched Ajax's shoulders relax. "When I saw your location, I was scared as hell I would find you dead. I brought

171

a team, thinking I couldn't find you like that again. If I did—" Ajax shook his head. He didn't finish his thoughts.

The confession didn't surprise Lucas as much as it should have. Lucas had changed when his life did. He didn't feel as mentally strong any longer. Lucas had lost part of himself in that alley. Even though he hadn't gone there for the reason he gave, Lucas couldn't say he wasn't sort of searching for answers. He hadn't found them. Lucas discovered something else. He wasn't alone any longer. His life was nothing like it had been before that night. Just like he had then, Ajax had come for him. Lucas understood now Ajax always would. They had each other.

Ajax pulled into Lucas' usual spot in the garage. Neither of them made any attempt to get out of the car. The leather seats of Lucas' Lexus seemed extra cozy in their silence. They held each other's stare. It seemed as if there should be a million things to say. Instead, they leaned toward each other. Their lips met. It was the sweetest and sexiest kiss Lucas had ever experienced. Their lips seemed to barely brush, even as they parted. It was like they just wanted to share the same air. The light touch had Lucas burning alive with desire. He never wanted to move. Unfortunately, they couldn't stay in the car forever.

Ajax pressed his forehead against Lucas's. His eyes stayed closed like he savored Lucas' space. "We should go inside."

"Yeah."

They reluctantly moved away and stepped from the car. Hand in hand, they headed inside. Lucas hadn't cleared the mudroom before his mom appeared.

She looked adorable, with her hair in a messy ponytail. Her ripped jeans and soft shirt made her look closer to her age. The walker fooled people. His mom was only forty-three. Since he was twenty-seven and her health had failed her, people automatically assumed she was older. But her looks hadn't faded, and she glowed since she had her freedom back.

"There you are. I've been looking for you everywhere. You didn't answer my calls."

Damn. "Yeah. Sorry. I turned my phone off earlier. I guess I forgot to turn it back on. What's up? Is everything okay?"

"Yeah. I just wanted to know if you wanted to go to dinner. Just the two of us," she tacked on.

Lucas glanced Ajax's way.

He flashed Lucas a sweet smile. "Go. I'll still be here when you get back."

Any other time, Lucas would be thrilled to spend some one-on-one time with his mom. Things still felt off tonight, but he would do anything to keep his mom smiling.

He pasted on a bright smile as he met his mom's stare again. "Sure. Grab your stuff and we'll go."

She shrugged. "I'm good. All I need is to slip on my shoes on the way out the door."

Lucas made a path for her to push through and step into her slip-on Vans. He cast another longing look Ajax's way.

Ajax kissed his forehead. "Seriously. I'll still be waiting. Have fun."

Lucas nodded. "I love you."

If he wasn't mistaken, Lucas swore tears filled Ajax's eyes again. He blinked them away before Lucas knew for sure. "I love you too. Be careful."

Lucas nodded and helped his mom out the door. It was second nature for him to get his mom settled in the passenger seat before folding her walker and stashing it in the back seat. He didn't say anything until they were pulling from the driveway.

"Okay. Tell me what's wrong."

Wendy laughed. "Nothing is wrong. It just seems like we never get to spend time alone together anymore. Plus, all they eat is that fancy-ass food. Don't get me wrong. The cooking is always delicious, but I'm not built that way. I want a greasy burger and bad-for-me fries. Let's hit a drive-thru and just eat in the car. We can park and chat—like we used to when you were a kid, and I got paid on Fridays."

Lucas loved that idea. It had always been just them. His mom had given birth to him at sixteen. She had dropped out of school and worked her ass off to support him. Lucas didn't even know who his father was. It was just them. His mom was amazing.

He pointed at an old-style restaurant where servers on skates brought food to car windows. "How about there?"

"Sounds great." His mom sounded extra happy tonight, but something about her mood seemed forced.

He didn't bring it up again until they had their food. "Okay. Seriously, Mom. What's going on with you tonight?"

Wendy dropped her gaze and toyed with a broken string from a hole in the knee of her jeans. "I've just been overthinking. You know how I am."

A strand of light red hair slipped from her ponytail. Lucas tucked it behind her ear. "You know you can talk to me about anything."

She flashed him a sweet smile. "I know. This is just a little uncomfortable for me."

That had Lucas' anxiety spiking. A nervous chuckle escaped him. "Come on.

There's no such thing as awkward between us. I'm pretty sure we've talked about things that would horrify any other mother."

Wendy laughed. "It was probably wrong of me to have such a close friendship with you your whole life. You've always been such an amazing kid. I never had to be one of those, 'I'm not one of your little friends' mom."

Lucas chuckled. "Yeah. You've always been such an amazing mom. I've never had to act out. I always had the attention other kids wanted."

A sad smile touched Wendy's lips. "That's the problem. I don't think I've been that great of a mom lately. When you wanted to leave Noir's, I should've stood my ground and left. I feel like I've been really selfish lately."

Lucas snorted. "You don't know how to be selfish, and I'm grown, Mom. You're allowed to be happy and free. It's your time to shine. You don't need to think of me first anymore."

It was Wendy's turn to snort. "Parenting doesn't end when your kids become adults. You'll always be first." She visibly swallowed. "Izaak kissed me."

Lucas wasn't surprised—like not even a little. He had seen the way Izaak doted on her. Assigned guard or not, his attention went way beyond duty. He prayed Noir hadn't turned his manipulations toward his mom. Still, Lucas nodded. He trusted his mom to see through people's scheming. She was the best judge of character he had ever known. "Did you not want him to kiss you?" If she said no, Lucas was fully prepared to call her on her bullshit. He had seen those heated looks tossed both ways.

A small smile touched Wendy's lips and slipped away. "It just got me to thinking. I don't want to start anything if you don't want to live under Noir's roof. It's totally understandable for you not to want to live in another man's house. You are valid for wanting to stand on your own and have the privacy of your own place."

Lucas held her stare. "Mom. I literally died working for that man. The least he can give me is a roof."

"You got hit by a car." Her eyes sparkled with laughter.

Lucas shrugged. He knew he had to keep up that lie, but still. "It happened while working for him on a night he was being extra demanding. It was Christmas, for fuck's sake. I missed that amazing marshmallow pistachio thing you always make. There's not enough he can do to make up for that."

Wendy gently slapped his arm as she laughed. "Stop."

Lucas' smile never dimmed as he watched her. She looked truly happy for the first time in Lucas' life. He could take away her guilt. "Besides, Ajax asked me to marry him and he's Noir's general. He can't leave."

"What?" Wendy's screeched question nearly blew out Lucas' eardrums. "Why didn't you say anything? Why didn't you lead with that? This is so, so amazing. I'd been hoping you'd finally found the one. The way he looks at you, sigh. You should've seen him when he started planning your surprise party. He was like a kid, all excited to make you happy. That man worships you. That's the kind of love you don't let get away."

There was no way Wendy could know how deep her words went with him. She gave him the outside insight he desperately required right when he needed it the most. "Yeah. I haven't said yes yet."

The look of irritation his mom gave him had him fighting back laughter. "Why not?" Her expression cleared. "Wait. He is good to you, right? I know no one can really know how someone else's relationship is behind closed doors. Am I wrong? Does he treat you right?"

The image of tears streaking down Ajax's face floated through his mind, solidifying his emotions. "Yeah. He loves me. The proposal just caught me so off guard. It wasn't one of those on his knee with a ring proposals. More or less, he just demanded I marry him in passing conversation."

A bark of laughter burst from Wendy. "That doesn't surprise me at all. He looks like a man used to always snapping his fingers and watching everyone fall in line. I suppose that's due to his position. He can't afford disobedience."

Lucas nodded along. "I plan to say yes."

Wendy clapped and squealed. She tried stealing a hug while not dumping the food from her lap. "I'm so happy for you two. You're so perfect together." She pulled away and turned serious in an instant. "Make him squirm a little, though. Twenty-four hours a day general or not, you don't ask someone to marry you without a ring."

Lucas was more than certain that happened all the time, but he appreciated her looking out for him. He watched her happily eat her fries, and the clouds parted. This was what he had always dreamed for them. Lucas hadn't dared to hope this would ever happen. He hadn't seen a path to watching Wendy thrive and find love while he broke free from the prison that was running drugs. Not only had he officially gotten out, but he had found love too. An amazing love that stood between him and the ugly life that had damn near put him in the ground.

He would say yes. Lucas couldn't imagine being anywhere else.

The glass shook in Ajax's hand as he tossed back his third shot. He couldn't recall ever feeling this close to breaking down. His insides still quivered so badly, he felt sick. Lucas had acted like they would move past this. Unfortunately, his mind betrayed him. Had Lucas texted his mom and set up this dinner alone so they could run? He hated the way he felt. Ajax didn't know how long it would take for him to feel normal again, but Lucas immediately leaving his sight didn't improve anything. All Ajax could do was trust him.

That meant believing he was worthy of Lucas. That would never happen.

Someone knocked on his closed bedroom door.

Ajax tossed back another shot. "Enter."

When the door opened, he was more than a little surprised to see Noir stepping inside. Noir wasn't the type to knock, especially in his own home.

"I heard you were back." He tilted his head toward the open liquor and shot glass in front of Ajax. "I see you've decided to get trolleyed. Did things not go well?"

Ajax didn't doubt for a second that Noir knew exactly what happened, down to every word they spoke. He played along, hoping Noir showed his hand. "I'm still not totally sure. He came home with me but immediately left with Wendy to get dinner."

Noir moved to the couch and sat. "I'm not surprised. Wendy has been pacing the house all day, trying to find Lucas."

That didn't set Ajax at ease. He took another shot.

Noir cocked his head and studied Ajax. "It's not like me to apologize, but you have me wondering if I should."

A humorless laugh burst from Ajax. "Why? You're not sorry."

Noir's cool expression never even twitched. "Of course I'm not. That doesn't make you any less important to me."

Unfortunately, Ajax knew that. He understood Noir like no one else did. That likely even included his husband. Ajax had watched Noir grow up. He knew exactly how much neglect it took to forge someone into having what it took to rule. Noir didn't apologize because he was a true prince through and through. Princes don't say they're sorry.

Ajax nodded toward the bottle. "Would you like a drink?"

Noir shook his head. "You shouldn't have another either. When Lucas comes home, you'll need to be on your toes."

Defying his prince, Ajax took another shot. His throat burned as he spoke. "If he comes home."

"Why wouldn't he? He loves you and I'm sure he knows by now that I only meant to rile you. Not ruin your relationship."

"Yeah. I'd like to hear the answer to that."

Ajax's gaze shot toward the door at Lucas' question. He had no idea how long Lucas stood there, but he had obviously been there long enough to hear Ajax admit he wasn't sure if Lucas would come back.

Noir stood. "My husband is waiting. I should get back to him."

Despite everything else happening, Ajax's chest still warmed at the way Noir and Lazarus loved each other. They were never apart and never tired of each other. Ajax wanted that too. With Lucas.

Lucas didn't speak again until they were alone. He crossed the room and leaned against the bar. His gaze dropped to the shot glass. "Seriously. Why did you think I wouldn't come back?" He met Ajax's stare. His sexy as fuck amber eyes melted every wall Ajax ever possessed.

Honesty was the only answer if he wanted to keep Lucas. "If it were me, I might not have because I know myself. I'm unbending. You'll always live under my thumb. I never faked a damn thing, but I am..." Ajax fought for the best description. "Difficult." That was all Ajax could think to say.

Lucas' mouth turned up in one corner. "You're spicy. I love that about you."

Ajax tilted his head back and blinked at the ceiling for a second, trying to recover from the sheer terror of almost losing Lucas.

Lucas fingered the sleeve of Ajax's dress shirt. "When you roll your sleeves like this and show off your sexy forearms, that shit gets me hot as hell. In fact, the first time I saw you this way, I swore you'd be mine one day."

Ajax met Lucas' stare. He looked serious. Like the conversation meant something to him. "I remember you teasing me for dressing down and slumming it. Derelict of duty, I believe you called it. But that was probably at least four or five years ago."

Lucas' gaze never wavered. "I know. Since the day Noir brought me on at nineteen, I've wanted you. But I knew I was too young, and you didn't look at me that way. I remember exactly when the way you look at me changed. You rushed me here after I'd been ordered to make an example of that one guy who still stays at least one payment behind. I was covered in blood and—for whatever reason—you panicked, rushing to get me clean. You practically ripped the shirt off my back. Then everything seemed to freeze. It was like a spark lit in you that finally matched the one I'd been carrying. From then on, I couldn't bring myself to truly settle down with anyone. No one else was you."

Ajax saw and felt the honesty behind every word. Maybe they had never been only friends. "That's not when I noticed you. In fact, there were times I had to force myself not to look your way. You were too young. Still are, honestly.

It's when you got serious with Jamison. That's when I stopped caring about your age. You should probably know all my sins now." Ajax took a breath. "I was the one who suggested Noir get Jamison involved. I'm the one who pointed out how useful he could be with his inside knowledge of some of our biggest clients. You weren't supposed to be with him. I had to make him go away. You've always been mine."

To his surprise, Lucas didn't react. He didn't blow up or walk away. "I know. When Noir told me to steal Jamison's client information, I knew it was you. You're the only one I ever talked to about anything related to Jamison. Very few people even knew what Jamison did back then, but you knew. I hated his job, which was so fucking dumb since I knew we weren't meant to be. Still, you're the only person I ever told."

Ajax had expected Lucas would be shocked. Instead, it was him. "If you knew, why didn't you confront me? I'm the reason you two split. I ruined your relationship on purpose. That's how greedy I am."

Lucas held his stare, giving Ajax a clear shot of the honesty in Lucas' every word. "Because you're my best friend. No matter how I felt about Jamison, I've never cared about anyone more than you, except for my mom. Maybe I never would've acted on things if I hadn't gotten attacked, but it's always been you."

Ajax felt humbled beyond words. Truly, he didn't know what to say. Even after everything that had come to light today,

Lucas still chose Ajax. He didn't deserve it. That didn't mean he wouldn't take it. Like Ajax had said, he was greedy. He always took what he wanted. This one time, though, he needed to know Lucas wanted this every bit as badly as him. It seemed he did, and it took every ounce of strength Ajax possessed not to break down. Since Lucas died while holding his hand, Ajax had been on such an exhausting rollercoaster of emotions. Thankfully, his body seemed to know what to do, even with his brain finally breaking under the weight of everything.

Ajax shuffled closer and boxed Lucas in against the bar. He stared into the eyes of the man who meant everything to him. Ajax would burn the world for this. "I want to be inside you."

Lucas' eyebrows rose. "In."

Ajax almost chuckled at Lucas' immediate agreement. Lucas hadn't even thought about it. He just agreed, like he had been waiting for Ajax to say just that. They hadn't flipped roles before now. He wasn't someone who believed in strict bedroom positions. Ajax hadn't pressed for this before because he absolutely loved riding Lucas' dick. But he needed to make love to Lucas, and Lucas was way too aggressive in the bedroom to move slowly.

Ajax moved in for a kiss before Lucas changed his mind. Lucas buried his hands in Ajax's hair and held on. Their mouths clashed and played. Ajax maneuvered Lucas toward the bed. At the edge, he grabbed two handfuls of Lucas' ass and lifted him from his feet just long enough to toss him onto the bed before immediately covering Lucas' body with his. They went right back to making out. They awkwardly stripped each other, fighting to get closer and never break their kiss. When their nude bodies came together, Ajax growled with possessiveness. This man was his. Lucas had no idea exactly how dangerous Ajax was. There was nowhere he could hide where Ajax wouldn't find him.

In his frenzied state, Ajax dove for the bedside table. His hands shook as he rolled a condom down his length. Lucas visibly fought for air while he watched Ajax suit up.

"You're so goddamn stunning." Ajax couldn't help the words. Lucas deserved them. The scars from his attack meant nothing. The red hair that covered his body in all the right places made Ajax hot as hell. Lucas had the most gorgeous eyes Ajax had ever seen. They were almost yellow. Unique, just like the man.

"There's no reason to flatter me. I'm more than willing. Hell, I was more than ready since our first kiss, but I didn't think my body could take it with everything I lost and whatnot. But I don't think it's possible for me to ever feel bad enough to say no to you." His fingertips skimmed Ajax's stomach in the lightest touch before they barely brushed Ajax's cock. Lucas looked turned on and hungry as hell. He was fucking killing Ajax. Ajax genuinely wanted to go slow and show Lucas the love he deserved.

"I wish you could see how you look at me."

Ajax couldn't bring himself to smile. "I don't have to see. I feel the way my love for you overtakes everything. There's no way it's not pouring from my eyes. Sometimes, the way I feel about you is too much and has nowhere to go. I imagine there isn't a soul who sees me looking at you and doesn't know you're my entire bloody world."

"Same. I can't wait to be your husband."

Those proved to be the words that broke Ajax. Before Ajax gathered a single wit, he already had Lucas lubed and ready. It wasn't until he felt Lucas' body give way, accepting him, that Ajax regained his sanity. This was Lucas. His earlier words rang in Ajax's ears. Ajax couldn't be rough with him. Lucas had lost organs, had a few spliced back together, or shortened. He only had one kidney now and his spleen was gone. Ajax wondered if he still lived in silent pain every day. Hurting Lucas was the one thing Ajax couldn't do.

He stole sweet kisses while rocking inside Lucas. The soft sounds Lucas made punched Ajax right in the heart. This was exactly what he wanted. Lucas had to feel how much Ajax loved him. Anything less was unacceptable.

A whimper vibrated against Ajax's lips. Lucas squirmed beneath him. "Ajax?"

"No." The breathless denial popped from him without even thinking. He wouldn't give in and fuck Lucas hard. "You can and will come like this."

"I'm greedy too." The whispered confession nearly broke Ajax.

"Then show me how much you want it. Let me watch you blow."

Lucas whined. He sounded as needy as he claimed to be. There were so many sides to Lucas. He could be caustic and unserious as hell. Lucas could turn wicked and teasing any second. But Ajax craved this side—the one only he got to see. He loved watching him writhe.

"That's it, beautiful." Ajax feared he might coax himself straight into an orgasm at this point. He couldn't stop talking. "I want that cum on my skin. I wish like hell I could make you drip with my juices. You look so goddamn delicious on my dick. I could stay right here forever." Pressure tightened Ajax's balls and climbed his shaft. He was dangerously close to finishing before Lucas. "You'll be my husband soon. Will you let me pump you full of cum after we're married? Can I fuck you raw?"

A strangled cry tore from Lucas. His body jerked so hard, Ajax was the one who nearly hurt himself. Stars popped in his vision. The way Lucas' body squeezed him had Ajax gasping for air, trying to breathe through the bliss that rocked his soul. Ecstasy kept pulling wave after wave from him. All Ajax could do was desperately kiss Lucas and beg any deity listening to let him live out his days just like this. They were more than best mates who fell in love. They were soulmates. Ajax knew that to his core.

Kash sat in darkness and savored the silence. Sometimes his mind could be so loud, he thought he might go deaf. The day had been enlightening. Kash knew his time was up in Atlantic City. He couldn't risk Lucas telling anyone about the out Ajax had given him. Too many people's lives were at stake. Kash wouldn't risk his family like that. Plus, Kash was restless. The nightlife was always hopping in Atlantic City, but everything had felt bland to Kash for a long time. He wasn't the type to stay in one place for long.

Kash's phone rang. He checked the face. Steel's name stared back at him. He had known this call would come. Just as he had known Lucas wouldn't leave Ajax. Even a blind man could see what was happening between those two. If Lucas had gotten the chance to skip out, Ajax would never stop hunting him. The general was terrifying on a good day. When crossed, he was nearly equal to the prince, and that guy was full-on insane.

Steel answered and tapped the speakerphone. "Hey, cousin. What's up?"

"I thought you'd want to know I never heard from your friend."

"Honestly, I'm not all that surprised. He didn't have the look of a true runner. But I had to offer an out, you know."

"I do. Unfortunately, I'm still short a guy. I guess I'll start making calls."

Kash didn't hesitate. "I'll do it."

Silence met his offer. Finally, Steel cleared his throat. "Are you sure?"

Kash stood, ready to head out that minute. "Send me the info."

"It's Ledger."

Kash immediately sat. He fiddled with his phone. "Well. There's a name I haven't heard in a long time."

"Should I find someone else?"

"No." Kash cleared his throat when his response came out sounding weird. "No," he repeated, hoping to hang on to his pride. "I'll do it."

Silence grew between them until it was uncomfortable. Steel finally broke it. "If you change your mind, I'm just one phone call away."

Kash stiffened his spine. "I've got it. Send me the deets."

"Okay." Steel did not sound like it was okay. "Everything is headed your way. Good luck."

A bark of laughter unexpectedly burst from Kash. Steel sounded like he sent Kash to his death. Maybe he did. Maybe Kash was ready.

CHAPTER TWELVE

THE ROOM SPUN SLIGHTLY, making Lucas realize he held his breath. The gorgeous chandeliers surrounding them seemed to dim. Lucas needed to take a damn breath.

"By the power of your king, you are tied for life."

Air rushed into his lungs. He saw Ajax's huge smile before Ajax kissed him. He didn't hold back. It didn't seem to matter to him that they stood before what felt like the whole damn population of The Republic of Serveno. A cheer rang out around them. The moment Ajax set him free, Lucas' gaze found his mom. They held each other's stare. A double wedding seemed so fitting for them. A team to the end. His mom winked and Izaac swept her from her feet, being mindful of her full gown before heading back down the aisle. Lucas took Ajax's arm and did the same. They followed Izaac back down the aisle. This time, they walked beneath raised swords. The guards Lucas had known since he started working for Noir smiled brightly, while the king's guard kept their stoic expressions.

Time seemed to slip away from him. Sharing the day with Izaac and Wendy took some of the pressure from Lucas' shoulders. Dinner and toasts flew past him before the dancing and mingling began. People kept bowing their heads as they passed. Lucas lasted an hour before he couldn't take it any longer.

"Why do people keep lowering their gaze? I'm getting sort of freaked out."

Ajax laughed. He kissed Lucas' temple. "I love you." Ajax made the claim with heavy laughter in his voice.

"I love you too." Lucas sounded as petulant as he felt. "Don't make fun of me for not understanding anything about this place."

Ajax's smile didn't dim. "I'm not. You just have that pouty expression I love so much. Ask any questions you want. This is your country too now."

That was true. While they had done the whole in front a judge thing in the U.S., due to Ajax's high position of power, he was required by the king to be officially married in his home country too. That way, if ever ordered home, Lucas would have no trouble coming with him.

Another person lowered their eyes.

Lucas sighed.

Ajax rubbed his back. "You married the general of the Royal Guard." Ajax took a sip of his champagne. His gaze skimmed the crowd. "And I'm like fifteenth in line for the throne."

Lucas' head whipped around. "What?"

Ajax flashed him a sweet smile.

Lucas blinked. He shouldn't have been surprised. He had known the queen had rescued Ajax from an abusive home. Lucas should have realized the royal family would never rescue some random child. Of course, he was part of the royals. "Well." Lucas blinked again, absorbing the news. "Why are they averting their gazes from me, though? I'm not in line for the throne. Right? Please tell me I'm not."

Ajax's laughing gaze swung his way. "No, but you're my husband. It would be considered untoward to not show you the same respect."

Lucas shook his head. "What else don't I know? Do I get beheaded if you leave me?"

It was Ajax's turn to shake his head. Then he went still and cocked his head to one side. "Actually, I probably should've said something early. There's no such thing as divorce here. You're stuck with me. At least in this country. While the people of Serveno are free to marry as many willing adults as they want, that's your spouse or spouses for life."

Lucas' chest hurt. "I mean, we're never getting divorced anyway, but you could take another husband?" There was no missing the hurt in Lucas' voice.

A line appeared between Ajax's eyebrows. "In theory, we could take another spouse. It would have to be something signed off by both spouses. However, none of that matters because I'll never touch anyone else and you won't live to gain a new spouse if I caught you cheating."

While Lucas realized Ajax had just threatened his life, Lucas still couldn't stop smiling. "Awww. I'd kill you too. You have nothing to worry about, though. I barely keep up with you. You're a nympho."

The bark of laughter Ajax released had heads turning their way.

Lucas couldn't stop smiling. He had never been happier. Hearing Ajax's laughter and seeing the happiness in Ajax's eyes was all Lucas lived for anymore.

"Don't be embarrassed. That's one of my favorite things about you. But I'm way too tired for anyone else. Seriously, you're sadistic. My back hurts all the time."

Ajax laughed so hard, no sound emerged. Lucas couldn't look away. He hadn't made a lot of good choices in his life, but Ajax was the best decision Lucas ever made. If they had never met, Lucas probably would have never married. Now he was fully prepared to be tied to this man for life. Ajax had saved him. In every way. Ajax was stuck now. Lucas would make sure he enjoyed the ride. Lucas smiled. He should have made that part of his vows. There was nothing quite like shocking an entire kingdom. Lucas fully intended to be scandalous his entire life. Thankfully, Ajax loved that about him. Their life together would be a happy one.

Keep an eye out for more...

About the Author

CHARITY PARKERSON IS AN award-winning and multi-published author with several companies. Born with no filter from her brain to her mouth, she decided to take this odd quirk and insert it in her characters. One of her greatest loves is writing morally gray characters. You'll find them scattered throughout her hundreds of titles.

*Nine-time Readers' Favorite Award Winner

*2015 Passionate Plume Award Finalist

*2013 Reviewers' Choice Award Winner

*2012 ARRA Finalist for Favorite Paranormal Romance

*Five-time winner of The Mistress of the Darkpath

Connect with her online:

*Sign up for her newsletter: https://bit.ly/charityparkersonnewsletter

*Join her readers' group on Facebook: http://bit.ly/CharitysTribe

*Website: https://www.charityparkerson.com

*A list of her social media accounts and giveaways all in one place: http://hy.page/charityparkerson

www.ingramcontent.com/pod-product-compliance
Lightning Source LLC
Chambersburg PA
CBHW070731280626
47159CB00023B/3088